W9-AND-276

SANDRA BROWN

RICOCHET

SIMON & SCHUSTER
New York   London   Toronto   Sydney

SIMON & SCHUSTER
Rockefeller Center
1230 Avenue of the Americas
New York, NY 10020

This book is a work of fiction.
Names, characters, places, and incidents
either are products of the author's imagination
or are used fictitiously. Any resemblance to
actual events or locales or persons, living or dead,
is entirely coincidental.

Copyright © 2006 by Sandra Brown Management Ltd.

All rights reserved,
including the right of reproduction
in whole or in part in any form.

First Simon & Schuster trade paperback export edition 2006

SIMON & SCHUSTER and colophon are registered trademarks
of Simon & Schuster, Inc.

For information about special discounts for bulk purchases,
please contact Simon & Schuster Special Sales at
1-800-456-6798 or business@simonandschuster.com.

Designed by Jaime Putorti

Manufactured in the United States of America

10   9   8   7   6   5   4   3   2   1

Library of Congress Cataloging-in-Publication Data

Brown, Sandra.
    Ricochet / Sandra Brown.
      p.   cm.
    1. Mystery—fiction.   I. Title.
  PS3552.R718 R53   2006
  813'.54—dc22   2006047351

ISBN-13: 978-1-4165-3235-4
ISBN-10:   1-4165-3235-8

ACKNOWLEDGMENTS

Savannah, Georgia, not only has some of the best food and most beautiful scenery in the continental United States, its people are the nicest. Among them are Major Everett Regan of the Savannah–Chatham Metropolitan Police Department, who gave of his valuable time to answer myriad questions. Ellen Winters went out of her way to assist me when I was relying strictly on "the kindness of strangers." Without the help of these professionals, getting the necessary details would have been much more difficult.

I'm also indebted to Cindy Moore, to whom Southern hospitality isn't just a catchphrase. She exemplifies it, and then goes above and beyond. Thank you, friend, for opening doors.

And, for exploring with me every square, every street, toting camera gear and risking life and limb to take requested photographs, without complaining—too much—of the heat and humidity . . . thank you, Michael.

Sandra Brown

RICOCHET

PROLOGUE

THE RECOVERY MISSION WAS CALLED OFF AT 6:56 P.M.
The grim announcement was made by Chief of Police
Clarence Taylor during a locally televised press conference.

His somber expression was in keeping with his buzz haircut and
military bearing. "The police department, along with all the other
agencies involved, devoted countless hours to the search in hope of a
rescue. Short of that, a recovery.

"However, since the exhaustive efforts of law enforcement officers, the Coast Guard, and civilian volunteers haven't produced any
encouraging evidence in several days, we've come to the sad conclusion that to continue an organized search would be futile."

The lone drinker at the bar, watching the snowy TV screen
mounted in the corner, tossed back the whiskey remaining in his
glass and motioned the barkeep for a refill.

The barkeep held the open bottle poised above the highball
glass. "You sure? You're hitting it pretty hard, pal."

"Just pour."

"Have you got a ride home?"

The question was met with a menacing glare. The barkeep
shrugged and poured. "Your funeral."

No, not mine.

Off the beaten path in a low-rent area of downtown Savannah,
Smitty's attracted neither tourists nor respectable locals. It wasn't

the kind of watering hole one came to seeking fun and frivolity. It didn't take part in the city's infamous pub crawl on St. Patrick's Day. Pastel drinks with cute names weren't served.

The potables were ordered straight up. You might or might not get a lemon twist like the ones the barkeep was mindlessly peeling as he watched the television news bulletin that had preempted a *Seinfeld* rerun.

On the TV screen, Chief Taylor was commending the tireless efforts of the sheriff's office, canine unit, marine patrol and dive team, on and on, blah, blah, blah.

"Mute that, will you?"

At the request of his customer, the barkeep reached for the remote control and silenced the TV. "He's dancing around it 'cause he has to. But if you cut through all the B.S., what he's saying is, the body's fish food by now."

The drinker propped both elbows on the bar, hunched his shoulders, and watched the amber liquor sloshing in his glass as he slid it back and forth between his hands across the polished wood surface.

"Ten days after going into the river?" The barkeep shook his head with pessimism. "No way a person could survive. Still, it's a hell of a sad thing. Especially for the family. I mean, never knowing the fate of your loved one?" He reached for another lemon. "I'd hate to think of somebody I loved, dead or alive, being in the river or out there in the ocean, in this mess."

He used his chin to motion toward the bar's single window. It was wide, but only about eighteen inches deep, situated high on the wall, much closer to the ceiling than to the floor, providing a limited view of the outside if one cared to look. It allowed only a slash of semi-light to relieve the oppressive gloom in the bar, and gave only a slim promise of hope to the hopeless inside.

A ponderous rain had been soaking the Low Country of Georgia and South Carolina for the last forty-eight hours. Unrelenting rain. Torrents of water falling straight down out of opaque clouds.

At times the rainfall had been so heavy that you couldn't see across the river to the opposite bank. Low-lying areas had become lakes. Roads had been closed due to flooding. Gutters roiled with currents as swift as white-water rapids.

The barkeep wiped lemon juice from his fingers and cleaned the blade of his knife on a towel. "This rain, can't say I blame 'em for calling off the search. They'll probably never find the body now. But I guess that means it'll forever remain a mystery. Was it murder or suicide?" He tossed aside his towel and leaned on the bar. "What do you think happened?"

His customer looked up at him with bleary eyes and said hoarsely, "I know what happened."

CHAPTER
1

Six Weeks Earlier

THE MURDER TRIAL OF ROBERT SAVICH WAS IN ITS FOURTH DAY. Homicide detective Duncan Hatcher was wondering what the hell was going on.

As soon as court had reconvened after the lunch break, the defendant's attorney, Stan Adams, had asked the judge for a private meeting. Judge Laird, as perplexed by the request as ADA Mike Nelson, had nonetheless granted it and the three had withdrawn to chambers. The jury had retired to the jury room, leaving only the spectators to question the significance of this unexpected conference.

They'd been out for half an hour. Duncan's anxiety grew with each passing minute. He'd wanted the trial to proceed without a blip, without any hitch that could result in an easy appeal or, God forbid, an overturned verdict. That's why this behind-closed-doors powwow was making him so nervous.

His impatience eventually drove him out into the corridor, where he paced, but never out of earshot of the courtroom. From this fourth-floor vantage point, he watched a pair of tugs guide a merchant ship along the channel toward the ocean. Then, unable to stand the suspense, he returned to his seat in the courtroom.

"Duncan, for heaven's sake, sit still! You're squirming like a two-year-old." To pass the time, his partner detective, DeeDee Bowen, was working a crossword puzzle.

"What could they be talking about in there?"

"Plea bargain? Manslaughter, maybe?"

"Get real," he said. "Savich wouldn't admit to a parking violation, much less a hit."

"What's a seven-letter word for surrender?" DeeDee asked.

"Abdicate."

She looked at him with annoyance. "How'd you come up with that so fast?"

"I'm a genius."

She tried the word. "Not this time. 'Abdicate' doesn't fit. Besides, that's eight letters."

"Then I don't know."

The defendant, Robert Savich, was seated at the defense table looking way too complacent for a man on trial for murder, and much too confident to allay Duncan's anxiety. As though feeling Duncan's stare on the back of his neck, Savich turned and smiled at him. His fingers continued to idly drum the arms of his chair as though keeping time to a catchy tune only he could hear. His legs were casually crossed. He was a portrait of composure.

To anyone who didn't know him, Robert Savich looked like a respectable businessman with a slightly rebellious flair for fashion. For court today he was dressed in a suit of conservative gray, but the slim tailoring of it was distinctly European. His shirt was pale blue, his necktie lavender. His signature ponytail was sleek and glossy. A multicarat diamond glittered from his earlobe.

The classy clothes, his insouciance, were elements of his polished veneer, which gave no indication of the unconscionable criminal behind them.

He'd been arrested and brought before the grand jury on numerous charges that included several murders, one arson, and various lesser felonies, most of which were related to drug trafficking. But over the course of his long and illustrious career, he'd been indicted and tried only twice. The first had been a drug charge. He'd been acquitted because the state failed to prove their case, which, granted, was flimsy.

His second trial was for the murder of one Andre Bonnet. Savich had blown up his house. Along with ATF agents, Duncan had investigated the homicide. Unfortunately, most of the evidence was circumstantial, but had been believed strong enough to win a conviction. However, the DA's office had assigned a green prosecutor who didn't have the savvy or experience necessary to convince all the jurors of Savich's guilt. The trial had resulted in a hung jury.

But it hadn't ended there. It was discovered that the young ADA had also withheld exculpatory evidence from attorney Stan Adams. The hue and cry he raised made the DA's office gun-shy to prosecute again in any sort of timely fashion. The case remained on the books and probably would until the polar ice caps melted.

Duncan had taken that defeat hard. Despite the young prosecutor's bungling, he'd regarded it a personal failure and had dedicated himself to putting an end to Savich's thriving criminal career.

This time, he was betting the farm on a conviction. Savich was charged with the murder of Freddy Morris, one of his many employees, a drug dealer whom undercover narcotics officers had caught making and distributing methamphetamine. The evidence against Freddy Morris had been indisputable, his conviction virtually guaranteed, and, since he was a repeat offender, he'd face years of hard time.

The DEA and the police department's narcs got together and offered Freddy Morris a deal—reduced charges and significantly less prison time in exchange for his boss Savich, who was the kingpin they were really after.

In light of the prison sentence he was facing, Freddy had accepted the offer. But before the carefully planned sting could be executed, Freddy was. He was found lying facedown in a marsh with a bullet hole in the back of his head.

Duncan was confident that Savich wouldn't escape conviction this time. The prosecutor was less optimistic. "I hope you're right, Dunk," Mike Nelson had said the previous evening as he'd coached Duncan on his upcoming appearance on the witness stand. "A lot hinges on your testimony." Tugging on his lower lip, he'd added thoughtfully, "I'm afraid that Adams is going to hammer us on the probable cause issue."

"I had probable cause to question Savich," Duncan insisted. "Freddy's first reaction to the offer was to say that if he even farted in our direction, Savich would cut out his tongue. So, when I'm looking down at Freddy's corpse, I see that not only is his brain an oozing mush, his tongue has been cut out. According to the ME, it was cut out while he was still alive. You don't think that gave me probable cause to go after Savich immediately?"

The blood had been fresh and Freddy's body still warm when Duncan and DeeDee were called to the grisly scene. DEA officers and SPD narcs were engaged in a battle royal over who had blown Freddy's cover.

"You were supposed to have three men monitoring his every move," one of the DEA agents yelled at his police counterpart.

"You had four! Where were they?" the narc yelled back.

"They thought he was safe at home."

"Yeah? Well, so did we."

"Jesus!" the federal agent swore in frustration. "How'd he slip past us?"

No matter who had botched the sting, Freddy was no longer any use to them and quarreling about it was a waste of time. Leaving DeeDee to referee the two factions swapping invectives and blame, Duncan had gone after Savich.

"I didn't plan on arresting him," Duncan had explained to Mike Nelson. "I only went to his office to question him. Swear to God."

"You fought with him, Dunk. That may hurt us. Adams isn't going to let that get past the jury. He's going to hint at police brutality, if not accuse you outright. False arrest. Hell, I don't know what all he'll pull out of the hat."

He'd ended by tacking on a reminder that nothing was a sure thing and that anything could happen during a trial.

Duncan didn't understand the ADA's concern. To him it seemed clear-cut and easily understood. He'd gone directly from the scene of Freddy Morris's murder to Savich's office. Duncan had barged in unannounced to find Savich in the company of a woman later identified by mug shots as Lucille Jones, who was on her knees fellating him.

This morning, Duncan's testimony about that had caused a hush to fall over the courtroom. Restless movements ceased. The bailiff, who had been dozing, sat up, suddenly wakeful. Duncan glanced at the jury box. One of the older women ducked her head in embarrassment. Another, a contemporary of the first, appeared confused as to the meaning of the word. One of the four male jurors looked at Savich with a smirk of admiration. Savich was examining his fingernails as though considering a manicure later in the day.

Duncan had testified that the moment he entered Savich's office, Savich had reached for a gun. "A pistol was lying on his desk. He lunged toward it. I knew I'd be dead if he got hold of that weapon."

Adams came to his feet. "Objection, Your Honor. Conclusion."

"Sustained."

Mike Nelson amended his question and eventually established with the jurors that Duncan had rushed Savich only to defend himself from possible harm. The ensuing struggle was intense, but finally Duncan was able to restrain Savich.

"And once you had subdued Mr. Savich," the prosecutor said, "did you confiscate that weapon as evidence, Detective Hatcher?"

Here's where it got tricky. "No. By the time I had Savich in restraints, the pistol had disappeared and so had the woman."

Neither had been seen since.

Duncan arrested Savich for assault on a police officer. While he was being held on that charge, Duncan, DeeDee, and other officers had constructed a case against him for the murder of Freddy Morris.

They didn't have the weapon that Duncan had seen, which they were certain Savich had used to slay Freddy Morris less than an hour earlier. They didn't have the testimony of the woman. They didn't even have footprints or tire prints at the scene because the tide had come in and washed them away prior to the discovery of the body.

What they did have was the testimony of several other agents who'd heard Freddy's fearful claim that Savich would cut out his tongue and then kill him if he made a deal with the authorities, or even talked to them. And, since Lucille Jones's whereabouts were unknown, Savich couldn't produce a credible alibi. The DA's office had won convictions on less, so the case had come to trial.

Nelson expected Duncan would get hammered by Savich's attorney during cross-examination that afternoon. Over lunch, he had tried to prepare him for it. "He's going to claim harassment and tell the jury that you've harbored a personal grudge against his client for years."

"You bet your ass, I have," Duncan said. "The son of a bitch is a killer. It's my sworn duty to catch killers."

Nelson sighed. "Just don't let it sound personal, all right?"

"I'll try."

"Even though it is."

"I said I'll try, Mike. But, yeah, it's become personal."

"Adams is going to claim that Savich has a permit to carry a handgun, so the weapon itself isn't incriminating. And *then* he's going to claim that there never was a weapon. He may even question if there was really a woman giving him a blow job. He'll deny, deny, deny, and build up a mountain of doubt in the jurors' minds. He may even make a motion to dismiss your entire testimony since there's no corroboration."

Duncan knew what he was up against. He'd come up against Stan Adams before. But he was anxious to get on with it.

He was staring at the door leading to the judge's chambers, willing it to open, when it actually did.

"All rise," the bailiff intoned.

Duncan shot to his feet. He searched the expressions of the three men as they reentered the courtroom and resumed their places. He leaned toward DeeDee. "What think you?"

"I don't know, but I don't like it."

His partner had an uncanny and reliable talent for reading people and situations, and she had just validated the foreboding he was feeling.

Another bad sign—Mike Nelson kept his head averted and didn't look in their direction.

Stan Adams sat down beside his client and patted the sleeve of Savich's expensive suit.

Duncan's gut tightened with apprehension.

The judge stepped onto the bench and signaled the bailiff to ask the jury to return. He took his seat behind the podium and carefully arranged his robe. He scooted the tray holding a drinking glass and a carafe of water one-half inch to his right and adjusted the micro-phone, which needed no adjustment.

Once the jury had filed in and everyone was situated, he said, "Ladies and gentlemen, I apologize for the delay, but a matter of im-portance had to be addressed immediately."

Cato Laird was a popular judge, with the public and with the media, which he courted like a suitor. Nearing fifty, he had the physique of a thirty-year-old and the facial features of a movie star. In fact, a few years earlier he had played a cameo role of a judge in a movie filmed in Savannah.

Comfortable in front of cameras, he could be counted on to pro-vide a sound bite whenever a news story revolved around crime, criminals, or jurisprudence. He was speaking in that well-known, often-heard silver-tongued tone now. "Mr. Adams has brought to my attention that during voir dire, juror number ten failed to dis-close that her son is enrolled in the next class of candidate officers for the Savannah–Chatham Metropolitan Police Department."

Duncan glanced at the jury box and noticed the empty chair in the second row.

"Oh, jeez," DeeDee said under her breath.

"The juror has admitted as much to me," Judge Laird said. "She didn't intentionally try to deceive the court, she simply failed to rec-ognize how that omission could affect the outcome of this trial."

"*What?*"

DeeDee nudged Duncan, warning him to keep his voice down.

The judge looked in their direction, but continued.

"When seating a jury, attorneys for each side have an opportu-nity to eliminate any individuals who they feel have the potential of swaying the verdict. Mr. Adams is of the opinion that a juror whose family member will soon become a police officer may have a funda-mental prejudice against any defendant in a criminal trial, but espe-cially one accused of this particularly egregious slaying."

He paused, then said, "I agree with counsel on this point and am therefore compelled to declare a mistrial." He banged his gavel. "Ju-rors, you are dismissed. Mr. Adams, your client is free to go. Court is adjourned."

Duncan came out of his chair. "You have got to be kidding!"

The judge's gaze sought him out and, in a tone that could have cut a diamond, he said, "I assure you I am not kidding, Detective Hatcher."

Duncan stepped into the aisle and walked up it as far as the railing. He pointed at Savich. "Your Honor, you cannot let him walk out of here."

Mike Nelson was at his elbow, speaking under his breath. "Dunk, calm down."

"You can retry the case, Mr. Nelson," the judge said as he stood and prepared to leave. "But I advise you to have more solid evidence before you do." He glanced at Duncan, adding, "Or more credible testimony."

Duncan saw red. "You think I'm *lying?*"

"Duncan."

DeeDee had come up behind him and taken hold of his arm, trying to pull him back down the aisle toward the exit, but he yanked his arm free.

"The pistol was real. It was practically smoking. The woman was real. She jumped to her feet when I came in and—"

The judge banged his gavel, silencing him. "You can testify at the next trial. If there is one."

Suddenly Savich was in front of him, filling his field of vision, smiling. "You blew it again, Hatcher."

Mike Nelson grabbed Duncan's arm to keep him from vaulting over the railing. "I'm gonna nail you, you son of a bitch. Etch it into your skin. Tattoo it on your ass. I'm gonna nail you."

His voice rife with menace, Savich said, "I'll be seeing you. Soon." Then he blew Duncan an air kiss.

Adams hastily ushered his client past Duncan, who looked toward the judge. "How can you let him go?"

"Not I, Detective Hatcher, the law."

"*You're* the law. Or rather you're supposed to be."

"Duncan, shut up," DeeDee hissed. "We'll redouble our search for Lucille Jones. Maybe the weapon will turn up. We'll get Savich sooner or later."

"We could have had him sooner," he said, making no attempt to lower his voice. "We could have had him today. We could have had him right fucking now if we'd had a judge who sides with cops more than he sides with criminals."

"Oh hell," DeeDee groaned.

"Detective Hatcher." Judge Laird leaned upon the podium and glared at Duncan. As though addressing him from a burning bush, he said, "I'm willing to do you a favor and overlook that statement because I understand the level of your frustration."

"You don't understand jack shit. And if you wanted to do me a favor, *Your Honor,* you would have replaced that juror instead of declaring a mistrial. If you wanted to do me a favor, you would have given us an even chance of putting this murderer out of commission for good."

Every muscle in the judge's handsome face tensed, but his voice remained remarkably controlled. "I advise you to leave this courtroom now, before you say something for which I'll be forced to hold you in contempt."

Duncan aimed his index finger at the exit door through which Savich and his attorney had just passed. "Savich is thumbing his nose at you, too, same as he is at me. He loves killing people, and you just handed him a free pass to go out and kill some more."

"I ruled as the law dictates."

"No, what you did—"

"Duncan, please," DeeDee said.

"—is crap on me. You crapped on the people who elected you because they believed your promise to be tough on criminals like Savich. You crapped on Detective Bowen here, and on the DA's office, and on everybody else who's ever tried to nail this bastard. That's what you did. Your Honor."

" 'Hands up.' "

"What?"

"Seven-letter word for surrender."

DeeDee gaped at Duncan as he situated himself in the passenger seat of her car and buckled his seat belt. "Forty-eight hours in jail, and that's the first thing you have to say?"

"I had a lot of time to think about it."

" 'Hands up' is two words, *genius.*"

"Still works, I bet."

"We'll never know. I threw the puzzle away."

"Couldn't finish?" he teased, knowing that it irked her because he could normally finish a puzzle long before she could. He had a knack for them; she didn't.

"No, I threw it away because I didn't want any reminders of your overplayed scene in the courtroom." She left the detention center parking lot and headed toward downtown. "You let your mouth overload your ass."

He sat brooding, saying nothing.

"Look, Duncan, I understand why you want Savich. We all want Savich. He's evil incarnate. But to verbally abuse a judge in his own courtroom? That's crazy. You damaged yourself as well as the department." She shot him a glance. "Of course it's not my place to lecture. You're the senior partner."

"Thank you for remembering that."

"I'm talking as your friend. I'm only saying this for your own good. Your zeal is admirable, but you've got to keep a rein on your temper."

Feeling not at all zealous, he stared moodily through the windshield. Savannah was baking under a fierce sun. The air was laden with moisture. Everything looked limp, wilted, as weary as he felt. The air conditioner in DeeDee's car was fighting a losing battle against the humidity. Already the back of his shirt was damp.

He wiped drops of sweat off his forehead. "I got a shower this morning, but I still stink like jail."

"Was it terrible?"

"Not too bad, but I don't want to go back any time soon."

"Gerard is unhappy with you," she said, speaking of Lieutenant Bill Gerard, their immediate supervisor.

"Judge Laird gives Savich a walk and Gerard is unhappy with *me?*"

DeeDee stopped at a traffic light and looked over at him. "Don't get pissed at what I'm about to say."

"I thought the lecture was over."

"You really gave the judge no choice." In the two years since DeeDee had been bumped up to homicide and made his partner, he'd never seen one iota of maternal instinct in her nature. Her expression now came close. "After the things you said, Judge Laird was practically duty-bound to hold you in contempt."

"Then His Honor and I have something in common. I feel bound to hold him in contempt, too."

"I think he got the message. As for Gerard, he has to toe the company line. He can't have his detectives telling off superior court judges."

"Okay, okay, I acknowledge the error of my ways. I served my time. At Savich's next trial, I promise to be a perfect gentleman, meek as a lamb, so long as Judge Laird, in turn, will cut us some slack. After the other day, he owes us."

"Uh, Duncan."

"Uh, what?"

"Mike Nelson called this afternoon." She hesitated, sighed. "The DA's position is that we didn't have enough on Savich—"

"I don't want to hear this, do I?"

"He said this trial was a long shot to start with, that we probably wouldn't have got a conviction anyway, and that he's not going to try the case again. Not unless we turn up something rock solid that places Savich at the scene."

Duncan had feared as much, but hearing it was worse than the dread of hearing it. He laid his head against the headrest and closed his eyes. "I don't know why I give a damn about Savich or any other scumbag. Nobody else does. The DA is probably more upset with me than he is with the Neanderthal who killed his wife last night over a tough pork chop. He was in the cell next to mine. If he told me once, he told me a dozen times that the bitch had it coming."

Sighing, he rolled his head to gaze out the window at the venerable live oaks along the boulevard. The clumps of Spanish moss dangling from their branches looked bedraggled in the oppressive heat.

"I mean, why do we bother?" he asked rhetorically. "If Savich pops a meth maker like Freddy Morris every now and then, he's performing a public service, isn't he?"

"No, because before that meth maker's body is cold, Savich will have his replacement set up for business."

"So, I repeat, what's the point? I'm all out of that zeal you referenced. I don't give a shit. Not anymore."

DeeDee rolled her eyes.

"Do you know how old I am?" he asked.

"Thirty-seven."

"Eight. And in twenty years I'll be fifty-eight. I'll have an enlarged prostate and a shrunken dick. My hair will be thinner, my waistline thicker."

"Your outlook gloomier."

"You're goddamn right," he said angrily, sitting up suddenly and jabbing the dashboard with his index finger as he enumerated his points. "Because I will have put in twenty more years of futility. There'll be more Saviches killing people. What will it all have been for?"

She pulled to the curb and braked. It hadn't registered with him until then that she'd driven him home, not to the parking lot where his car had been abandoned at the judicial center when he was taken into custody and marched from the courtroom.

DeeDee leaned back against her seat and turned to him. "Granted, we've had a setback. Tomorrow—"

"Setback? *Setback?* We're as dead as poor Freddy Morris. His execution scared the hell out of any other mule who has ever even remotely considered striking a deal with us or the Feds. Savich used Freddy to send a message, and it went out loud and clear. You talk, you die, and you die ugly. Nobody will talk," he said, enunciating the last three words.

He slammed his fist into his palm. "I cannot believe that slick son of a bitch got off again. How does he do it? Nobody's that supernaturally lucky. Or that smart. Somewhere along his body-strewn path, he must've struck a deal with the devil. All the demons in hell must be working for his side. But I swear this to you, DeeDee. If it's the last thing I do—" Noticing her smile, he broke off. "What?"

"Don't look now, Duncan, but you sound full of zeal again."

He grumbled a swear word or two, undid his seat belt, and pushed open the car door. "Thanks for the lift."

"I'm coming in." Before getting out, she reached into the backseat for the dry cleaner's bag that had been hanging on the hook on the door.

"What's that?"

"The suit I'm wearing tonight. I'm going to change here, save myself the drive all the way home and then back downtown."

"What's tonight?"

"The awards dinner." She looked at him with consternation. "Don't tell me you forgot."

He raked his fingers through his unruly hair. "Yeah, I did. Sorry, partner, but I'm just not up for that tonight."

He didn't want to be around cops tonight. He didn't want to face Bill Gerard in a semi-social setting, knowing that first thing tomorrow morning, he'd be called into his office for a good old-fashioned ass-chewing. Which he deserved for losing his cool in court. His outrage was justified, but he'd been wrong to express it then and there. What DeeDee had said was right—he'd hurt their cause, not helped it. And that must have given Savich a lot of satisfaction.

She bent down to pick up two editions of the newspaper from the sidewalk and swatted him in the stomach with them. "You're going to that dinner," she said and started up the brick steps to the front door of his town house.

Once the door was unlocked and they were inside, he made a beeline for the wall thermostat and adjusted the AC.

"How come your alarm wasn't set?" DeeDee asked.

"I keep forgetting the code."

"You never forget anything. You're just lazy. It's stupid not to set it, Duncan. Especially now."

"Why especially now?"

"Savich. His parting 'I'll see you. Soon,' resonated like a threat."

"I wish he would come after me. It would give me an excuse."

"To . . . ?"

"To do whatever was necessary." He flung his sport jacket onto a chair and made his way down the hallway toward the kitchen at the back of the house. "You know where the guest bedroom and bath are," he said, indicating the staircase. "Help yourself."

DeeDee was right on his heels. "You're going to that dinner with me, Duncan."

"No, what I'm going to do is have a beer, a shower, a ham sandwich with mustard hot enough to make my eyes water, and—"

"Play the piano?"

"I don't play the piano."

"Right," she said drolly.

"What I was going to say is that maybe I'll catch a ball game on TV before turning in early. Can't tell you how much I look forward to sleeping in my own bed after two nights on a jail cot. But what I am *not* going to do is get dressed up and go to that dinner."

She planted her hands on her hips. "You promised."

He opened his fridge and, without even looking, reached inside and took out a can of beer, popping the top and sucking the foam off the back of his hand. "That was before my incarceration."

"I'm receiving a commendation."

"Well deserved. Congratulations. You cracked the widow who cracked her husband over the head with a crowbar. Great instinct, partner. I couldn't be more proud." He toasted her with his can of beer, then tipped it toward his mouth.

"You're missing the point. I don't want to go to a fancy dinner alone. You're my escort."

He laughed, sputtering beer. "It isn't a cotillion. And since when do you care if you've got an *escort?* In fact, that's the first time I've ever heard you use that word."

"If I don't have an *escort,* the bubbas will give me hell. Worley and company will say I couldn't get a date if my life depended on it. You're my partner, Duncan. It's your duty to back me up, and that includes helping me save face with the yahoos I'm forced to work with."

"Call up that cop in the evidence room. What's his name? He gets flustered every time he looks at you. He'd escort you."

She frowned with distaste. "He's got a moist handshake. I hate that." Looking thoroughly put out, she said, "It's a few hours of your time, Duncan."

"Sorry."

"You just don't want to be seen with me."

"What are you talking about? I'm seen with you all the time."

"But never in a social setting. Some people there might not know

I'm your coworker. Heaven forbid anyone mistake me for your date. Being with a woman who's short, dumpy, and frizzy might damage your reputation as a stud muffin."

He set his beer on the countertop, hard. "Now you've made me mad. First of all, I don't have that reputation. Secondly, who says you're short?"

"Worley called me vertically challenged."

"Worley's an asshole. Nor are you dumpy. You're compactly built. Muscular, because you work out like a fiend. And your hair's frizzy because you perm the hell out of it."

"Makes it easy to take care of," she said defensively. "Keeps it out of my eyes. How'd you know it was permed?"

"Because when you get a fresh one, I can smell it. My mom used to give herself perms at home. Stunk up the whole house for days. Dad begged her to go to the beauty parlor, but she said they charge too much."

"Salon, Duncan. They're not called beauty parlors anymore."

"*I* know that. Mom doesn't."

"Do they know about your jail time?"

"Yeah," he said with some regret. "I used my one phone call to talk to them because they get nervous if they don't hear from me every few days. They're proud of what I do, but they worry. You know how it is."

"Well, not really," she said, using the sour tone of voice she used whenever her parents were referenced, even tangentially. "Do your folks know about Savich?" she asked.

He shrugged. "I downplay it."

"What did they think of their son being in jail?"

"They had to bail me out once when I was in high school. Underage drinking. I caught hell that time. This time, Dad commended me for standing up for what I thought was right. Of course I didn't tell him that I'd used the f-word to get my point across."

DeeDee smiled. "You're lucky they're so understanding."

"I know." In truth, Duncan did know how fortunate he was. DeeDee's relationship with her parents was strained. Hoping to divert her from that unhappy topic, he said, "Did I tell you that Dad's gone high-tech? Prepares his sermons on a computer. He has the whole Bible on software and can access any scripture with a keystroke. But not everybody is happy about it. One old-timer in his congregation is convinced that the Internet is the Antichrist."

She laughed. "He may be right."

"May be." He picked up his beer and took another drink.

"Not that I was asked, but I'd love a Diet Coke, please."

"Sorry." He opened the fridge and reached inside. Then, with a yelp, yanked back his hand. "Whoa!"

"What?"

"I've gotta remember to set my alarm."

DeeDee pushed him aside and looked into the refrigerator. She made a face, and, like Duncan, recoiled. "What *is* that?"

"If I were to guess, I'd say it's Freddy Morris's tongue."

CHAPTER

2

DUNCAN WOULD TAKE THE SEVERED TONGUE—NOW SEVERAL months old—to the ME in the morning. For the time being he placed it in an evidence bag and returned it to his refrigerator.

DeeDee was aghast. "You're not going to leave it in there, are you? With your *food?*"

"I don't want it smelling up my house."

"Are you going to have the place dusted for prints?"

"It wouldn't do any good and would only make a mess."

Whoever had been inside his house, either Savich or one of his many errand boys—Duncan guessed the latter—would have been too smart to leave fingerprints. More disturbing than finding the offensive, shriveled piece of tissue was knowing that his house had been violated. In and of itself, the tongue was a prank. Savich's equivalent to *na-na-na-na-na*. He was rubbing Duncan's nose in his defeat.

But the message it sent was no laughing matter. Duncan had detected the underlying threat in Savich's taunting good-bye, but this wasn't the retribution that threat foretold. This was only a prelude, a hint of things to come. It broadcast loud and clear that Duncan was vulnerable and that Savich meant business. By coming into Duncan's home, he'd taken their war to a new level. And only one of them would survive it.

Although he minimized his apprehension with DeeDee, he did not underestimate Savich and the degree of his brutality. When he launched his attack on Duncan, it would be merciless. What worried Duncan most was that he might not see it coming until it was too late.

He'd hoped the incident would relieve him of having to attend the awards dinner with DeeDee. Surely she wouldn't require him to go now. But she persisted, and ultimately he gave in. He dressed in a dark suit and tie and went with her to one of the major hotels on the river where the event was being held.

Upon entering the ballroom, he took a cursory glance at the crowd and stopped dead in his tracks. "I cannot believe this!" he exclaimed.

Following the direction of his gaze, DeeDee groaned. "I didn't know he was going to be here, Duncan. I swear."

Judge Cato Laird, immaculately attired and looking as cool as the drink in his hand, was chatting with police chief Taylor.

"I formally release you from your obligation," DeeDee said. "If you want to leave, you won't get an argument from me."

Duncan's eyes stayed fixed on the judge. When Laird laughed, the corners of his eyes crinkled handsomely. He looked like a man confident of the rightness of every decision he'd ever made in his entire life, from the choice of his necktie tonight to declaring Savich's murder trial a mistrial.

Duncan would be damned before he tucked tail and slunk out. "Hell no," he said to DeeDee. "I wouldn't pass up this chance to escort you when you're this gussied up. You're actually wearing a skirt. First time I've ever seen you in one."

"I swore off them once I graduated from Catholic high school."

He made a point of looking at her legs. "Better than decent. Fairly good, in fact."

"You're full of shit, but thanks."

Together they wove their way through the crowd, stopping along the way to speak to other policemen and to be introduced to significant others they hadn't met before. Several mentioned Duncan's days in jail, the sentiments ranging from anger to sympathy. He responded by joking about it.

When they were spotted by the police chief, Taylor excused himself from the group he was speaking with and approached them to extend his congratulations to DeeDee for the commendation she was to receive later that evening. While she was thanking him, someone addressed Duncan from behind.

Turning, he came face-to-face with Cato Laird, whose countenance was as guileless as that of the lead soprano in his dad's church choir. Reflexively Duncan's jaw clenched, but he replied with a civil, "Judge Laird."

"Detective. I hope there are no hard feelings." He extended his right hand.

Duncan clasped it. "For the jail time? I have only myself to blame for that."

"What about the mistrial?"

Duncan glanced beyond the judge's shoulder. Although DeeDee was being introduced to the mayor, who was enthusiastically pumping her hand, she was keeping a nervous eye on him and Laird. Duncan felt like telling the judge in the most explicit terms what he thought of his ruling and where he could shove his gavel.

But this was DeeDee's night. He would hold his temper. He would even refrain from telling the judge about the unpleasant surprise he'd had waiting in his home upon his return.

His eyes reconnected with the judge's dark gaze. "You know as well as I do that Savich is guilty of the Morris hit, so I'm certain you share my misgivings about releasing him." He paused to let that soak in. "But I'm equally certain that, under the circumstances, you ruled according to the law and your own conscience."

Judge Laird gave a slight nod. "I'm glad you appreciate the complexities involved."

"Well, I had forty-eight hours to contemplate them." He grinned, but if the judge had any perception at all, he would have realized that it wasn't a friendly expression. "Please excuse me. My partner is signaling for me to rejoin her."

"Of course. Enjoy the evening."

The judge stepped aside and Duncan brushed past him.

"What did he say?" DeeDee asked out the side of her mouth as Duncan took her arm and guided her toward the bar.

"He told me to enjoy the evening. Which I think includes having a drink."

He elbowed them through the crowd to the bar, ordered a bourbon and water for himself and a Diet Coke for her. Another detective in their division sidled up to them, awkwardly holding a drink in one hand and balancing a plate piled with hors d'oeuvres in the other.

"Hey, Dunk," he said around a mouthful of crab dip, "introduce me to your new squeeze."

"Eat shit and die, Worley," she said.

"What do you know? She sounds just like Detective Bowen!"

Worley was a good detective but one of the "yahoos" that DeeDee had referred to earlier. Never without a toothpick in his mouth, he held one there now, even as he ate from his plate of canapés. He and DeeDee had an ongoing contest to see who could better insult the other. The score was usually tied.

"Lay off, Worley," Duncan said. "DeeDee is an honoree tonight. Behave."

DeeDee was always in cop mode. Having worked with her for two years, Duncan thought that was possibly the only mode she operated in. Even tonight, despite the skirt and the lip gloss she'd smeared on for the occasion, she was thinking like a cop. "Tell Worley what we found in your house."

Duncan described the severed tongue. He indicated a chunk of meat on Worley's plate. "Looked sorta like that."

"Jeez." Worley shuddered. "How do you know Morris was the rightful owner?"

"Just a guess, but a pretty good one, don't you think? I'll take it to the lab tomorrow."

"Savich is pricking with you."

"He's a regular comedian, all right."

"But coming at you where you live . . ." Worley rearranged his toothpick and popped the questionable chunk of meat into his mouth. "That's ballsy. So, Dunk, you spooked?"

"He'd be stupid not to be a little spooked," DeeDee said, answering for him. "Right, Duncan?"

"I guess," he replied absently. He was wondering if, when the final showdown came, he would be able to kill Savich without compunction. He supposed he could, because he knew with certainty that Savich wouldn't hesitate to kill him.

In an effort to lighten the mood, Worley said, "Honest, DeeDee, you look sorta hot tonight."

"Little good it'll do you."

"If I get drunk enough, you might even start to look like a woman."

DeeDee didn't miss a beat. "Sadly, I could never get drunk enough for you to start looking like a man."

This was familiar office banter. The men in the Violent Crimes Unit gave DeeDee hell, but they all respected her skill, dedication, and ambition, all of which she had in surplus. When the situation called for it, the teasing stopped, and her opinions were respected equally with those of her male counterparts, sometimes more. "Women's intuition" was no longer just a catchphrase. Because of DeeDee's perception, they'd come to believe in it.

Knowing she could fend for herself without his help, Duncan turned away and let his gaze rove over the crowd.

Later, he remembered it was her hair that had first called her to his attention.

She was standing directly beneath one of the directional lights recessed into the ceiling thirty feet above her. It acted like a spotlight, making her hair look almost white, marking her as though she were the only blonde in the crowd.

It was in a simple style that bordered on severity—pulled back into a small knot at the nape of her neck—but it defined the perfect shape of her head and showed off the graceful length of her neck. He was admiring that pale nape when a nondescript woman who'd been blocking his view of the rest of her moved away. He saw her back. All of it. Tantalizing square inches of bare skin from her neck to her waist, even slightly below.

He didn't know jewelry could be worn on that part of the body, but there it was, a clasp made of what looked like diamonds winking at him from the small of her back. He imagined the stones would be warm from her skin.

Just from looking at her, his skin had turned warm.

Someone moved up behind her, said something. She turned, and Duncan got his first look at her face. Later, he thought that maybe his jaw had actually dropped.

"Dunk?" Worley nudged his arm. "You okay?"

"Yeah. Sure."

"I asked you how jail was."

"Oh, just peachy."

The other detective leaned toward him and leered. "You have to fight off any cell mates looking for romance?"

"No, they were all pining for you, Worley."

DeeDee laughed so suddenly, she snorted. "Good one, Duncan."

He turned away again, but the blonde had moved from the spot where he'd seen her. Impatiently his gaze scanned the crowd, until he located her again. She was talking to a distinguished-looking older couple and sipping a glass of white wine with seeming uninterest in both it and the conversation. She was smiling politely, but her eyes had a distant quality, like she wasn't quite connected to what was going on around her.

"You're drooling." DeeDee had moved up beside him and followed his stare to the woman. "Honestly, Duncan," she said with exasperation. "You're embarrassing yourself."

"Can't help it. I've fallen into instant lust."

"Rein it in."

"I don't think I can."

"Don't want to, you mean."

"Right, don't want to. I didn't know that getting struck by lightning could feel so good."

"Lightning?"

"Oh yeah. And then some."

DeeDee critically looked the woman over and shrugged. "She's okay, I guess. If you're into tall, thin, perfect hair, and flawless skin."

"To say nothing of her face."

She took a noisy sip of her Diet Coke. "Yeah, there's that. I gotta give credit where credit's due. As usual, your sexual radar homed in on the dishiest babe in the room."

He shot her his wicked smile. "It's this gift I have."

The couple moved away from the woman, leaving her standing by herself in the midst of the crowd. "The lady looks lost and lonely," Duncan said. "Like maybe she needs a big strong cop to come to her rescue. Hold my drink." He thrust his glass toward DeeDee.

"Have you lost your mind?" She stepped in front of him to block his path. "That would be the height of stupidity. I will not stand by and watch as you self-destruct."

"What are you talking about?"

DeeDee looked at him with sudden understanding. "Oh. You don't know."

"What?"

"She's married, Duncan."

"Shit. Are you sure?"

"To Judge Cato Laird."

"What did he say to you?"

Elise Laird set her jeweled handbag on the dressing table and stepped out of her sandals. Cato had come upstairs to their bedroom ahead of her. He was already undressed and in his robe, sitting on the side of their bed.

"Who?" she asked.

"Duncan Hatcher."

She pulled a pin from her hair. "Who?"

"The man you were talking to in the porte cochere. When I went to pay for the valet parking. Surely you remember. Tall, rugged, in dire need of a haircut, built like a wide receiver. Which he was. At Georgia, I believe."

"Oh, right." She dropped the hairpins next to her handbag and uncoiled the chignon, then combed her fingers through her hair. Facing the mirror, she smiled at her husband's reflection. "He asked if I had change. He needed to tip the parking valet and didn't have any bills smaller than a ten."

"He only asked for change?"

"Hmm." Reaching behind her she tried to undo the clasp of the diamond brooch at the small of her back. "Could you help me here, please?"

Cato left the bed and moved up behind her. He unfastened the clasp, pulled the pin from the black silk with care, then handed her the brooch and placed his hands on her shoulders, massaging gently. "Did Hatcher address you by name?"

"I honestly don't remember. Why? Who is he?"

"He's a homicide detective."

"Savannah police?"

"A decorated hero with a master's degree in criminology. He has brains and brawn."

"Impressive."

"Up till now he's been an exemplary officer."

"Till now?"

"He testified in my court this week. Murder trial. When circumstances forced me to declare a mistrial, he lost his temper. Became vituperative. I found him in contempt and sentenced him to two days in jail. He was released just this afternoon."

She laughed softly. "Then I'm sure he didn't know who I was. If he had, he would have avoided speaking to me." She took off her earrings. "Was the woman with him his wife?"

"Police partner. I don't believe he's married." He slipped the dress off Elise's shoulders, sliding the fabric down her arms, baring her to the waist. He studied her in the mirror. "I guess I can't blame the man for trying."

"He didn't *try* anything, Cato. He asked me for change."

"There were other people he could have asked, but he asked you." Reaching around her, he took the weight of her breasts in his palms. "I thought he might have recognized you, that you might have met before."

Meeting his dark eyes in the mirror, she said, "I suppose it's possible, but if so, I don't remember it. I wouldn't have remembered speaking to him tonight if you hadn't brought it up."

"Untrimmed dirty-blond hair isn't attractive to you? That shaggy, scruffy look doesn't appeal?"

"I much prefer graying temples and smoother shaves."

The zipper at the back of her dress was short. He smiled into the mirror as he pulled it down, following the cleft between her buttocks, then pushed the dress to the floor, leaving her in only a black lace thong. He turned her to face him. "This is the best part of these dull evenings out. Coming home with you." He looked at her, waiting. "No comment?"

"I have to say it? You know I feel the same."

Taking her hand, he folded it around his erection. "I lied, Elise," he whispered as he guided her motions. "This is the best part."

A half hour later, she eased herself from the bed, padded to the closet for a robe, and pulled it on. She paused briefly at her dressing table, then went to the door. It creaked when she pulled it open. She looked back toward the bed. Cato didn't stir.

She slipped from the room and tiptoed downstairs. Her insomnia concerned him. Sometimes he would come downstairs and find her on the sofa in the den, watching a DVD of one of her favorite movies. Sometimes she was reading in the living room, sometimes sitting in the sunroom, staring out at the lighted swimming pool.

He sympathized with her sleeplessness and urged her to get medication to help remedy it. He chided her for leaving their bed without waking him when he might have helped soothe her into sleep.

Recently she had begun to wonder if his concern was over the insomnia, or her nocturnal prowls through the house.

A night-light was left on in the kitchen, but the route was so familiar she could have found her way without it. Whatever else she did when she came downstairs, she always poured herself a glass of milk, which she claimed helped, and left the empty glass in the sink to ensure never being caught in a lie.

Standing at the sink, sipping the unwanted milk, she hoped that Cato would never catch her in the lie she'd told him tonight.

The detective *had* known who she was; he had called her by name.

"Mrs. Laird?"

When she turned, she was struck first by his height. Cato was tall, but Duncan Hatcher topped him by several inches. She had to tilt her head back to look into his face. When she did, she realized that he was standing inappropriately close, but not so close as to call attention to it. His eyes had the sheen of inebriation, but his speech wasn't slurred.

"My name is Duncan Hatcher."

He didn't extend his hand, but he looked down at hers as though expecting her to shake hands with him. She didn't. *"How do you do, Mr. Hatcher?"*

He had a disarming smile, and she suspected he knew that. He also had enough audacity to say, *"Great dress."*

"Thank you."

"I like the diamond clip at the small of your back."

She coolly nodded an acknowledgment.

"Is that all that's keeping it on?"

That was an improper remark. And so was the insinuation in his eyes. Eyes that were light gray and darkly dangerous.

"Good-bye, Mr. Hatcher."

She was about to turn away when he moved a step closer, and for a moment she thought he would touch her. He said, *"When are we going to see each other again?"*

"I beg your pardon?"

"When are we going to see each other again?"

"I seriously doubt we are."

"Oh, we are. See, every judge who finds me in contempt and sends me to jail? I make it a point to fuck his wife."

He made it sound like a promise. Shock rendered her speechless and motionless. So for several seconds they simply stood there and looked at each other.

Then two things happened simultaneously that broke the stare. The woman she now knew was his partner seized Duncan Hatcher by the arm and dragged him toward the car that a parking valet had just delivered. And Cato appeared in her peripheral vision. As he approached her, she turned toward him and managed to smile, although the muscles of her face felt stiff and unnatural.

Her husband looked suspiciously after Hatcher as the woman hustled him into the passenger seat of the car. Elise had feared Cato would confront her then about the brief exchange, but he hadn't. Not until they were home, and by then she'd had time to fabricate a lie.

But she wondered now why she had lied to her husband about it.

She poured the remainder of the unwanted milk down the drain and left the glass in the sink, where it would be conspicuous. Leaving the kitchen, she returned to the foot of the curving staircase in the foyer. There she paused to listen. The house was silent. She detected no movement upstairs.

Quickly she went down the center hallway and into Cato's study. She crossed the room in darkness, but once behind the desk, switched on the lamp. It cast dark shadows around the room, particularly onto the floor-to-ceiling bookshelves that formed the wall behind the desk.

She swung open the false shelf that concealed the wall safe and tried the handle, knowing already that it wouldn't budge. The safe was kept locked at all times, and even as they approached three years of marriage, Cato had never entrusted her with the combination.

She replaced the shelf of faux books and stepped back so she could study the bookcase wall as a whole. Then, as she'd done many times before, she broke it down into sections, focusing on one shelf at a time, letting her gaze slowly move from volume to volume.

There were countless hiding places in this bookshelf.

On a shelf slightly above her head, she noticed that one of the leather-bound volumes extended a fraction of an inch over the edge of the shelf. Coming up on tiptoe, she reached overhead to further investigate.

"Elise?"

She whipped around, gasping in fright. "Cato! Good Lord, you scared me."

"What are you doing?"

Her heart in her throat, she took the diamond pin from the pocket of her robe, where she'd had the foresight to place it before leaving the bedroom. "My brooch."

"Is that all that's keeping it on?"

It surprised her that her memory would replay Duncan Hatcher's suggestive remark at this moment, when her husband was looking at her curiously, waiting for an explanation.

"I was going to leave it here on your desk with a note so you'd see it before you left in the morning," she said. "I think some of the stones are loose. A jeweler should take a look."

He advanced into the room, looked at the pin lying in her extended palm, then into her eyes. "You didn't mention loose stones earlier."

"I forgot." She gave him a small, suggestive smile. "I got distracted."

"I'll take it downtown with me tomorrow and drop it off at the jeweler."

"Thank you. It's been in your family for decades. I'd hate to be responsible for losing one of the stones."

He looked beyond her at the bookcase. "What were you reaching for?"

"Oh, one of your volumes up there isn't lined up properly. I just happened to notice it. I know how finicky you are about this room."

He joined her behind the desk, reached up, and pushed the legal tome back into place. "There. Mrs. Berry must have dislodged it when she was dusting."

"Must have."

He placed his hands on her upper arms and rubbed them gently. "Elise?" he said softly.

"Yes?"

"Anything you want, darling, you only have to ask."

"What could I possibly want? I don't want for anything. You're extremely generous."

He looked deeply into her eyes, as though searching for something behind her steady gaze. Then he squeezed her arms quickly before releasing them. "Did you have your milk?" She nodded. "Good. Let's go back to bed. Maybe you'll be able to sleep now."

He waited for her to precede him. As she made her way toward the door, she glanced back. Cato was still standing behind his desk, watching her. The glare of the lamp cast his features into stark relief, emphasizing his thoughtful frown.

Then he switched off the lamp and the room went dark.

CHAPTER
3

DUNCAN DIDN'T NEED THE LIGHTS ON IN ORDER TO PLAY. In fact, he liked to play in the dark, when it seemed that the darkness produced the music and that it had no connection to him. It was sort of that way even with the lights on. Whenever he touched a piano keyboard, he relinquished control to another entity that lived in his subconscious and emerged only on those occasions.

"It's a divine gift, Duncan," his mother had declared when he tried to explain the phenomenon to her with the limited vocabulary of a child. "I don't know where the music comes from, Mom. It's weird. I just . . . I just *know* it."

He was eight when she had determined it was time to begin his music lessons. When she sat him down on their piano bench, pointed out middle C, and began instructing him on the fundamentals of the instrument, they discovered to their mutual dismay that he already knew how to play.

He hadn't known that he could. It shocked him even more than it did his astonished parents when he began playing familiar hymns. And not just picking out single-note melodies. He knew how to chord without even knowing what a chord was.

Of course, for as far back as he could remember, he'd heard his mother practicing hymns for Sunday services, which could have explained how he knew them. But he could also play everything else. Rock. Swing. Jazz. Blues. Folk songs. Country and western. Classical. Any tune he had ever heard, he could play.

"You play by ear," his mother told him as she fondly and proudly stroked his cheek. "It's a gift, Duncan. Be thankful for it."

Not even remotely thankful for it, he was embarrassed by his "gift." He thought of it more like a curse and begged his parents not to boast about it, or even to tell anybody that he had the rare talent.

He certainly didn't want his friends to know. They'd think he was a sissy, a dork, or a freak of nature. He didn't want to be gifted. He wanted to be a plain, ordinary kid. He wanted to play sports. Who wanted to play the stupid *piano?*

His parents tried to reason with him, saying it was okay for a person to play sports and also be a musician, and that it would be a shame for him to waste his musical talent.

But he knew better. He went to school every day, not them. He knew he'd be made fun of if anyone ever found out that he could play the piano and had tunes he didn't even know the names of stored up inside his head.

He held firm against their arguments. When pleading with them didn't work, he resorted to obstinacy. One night after a supper-long debate over it, he swore that he would never touch a keyboard again, that they could chain him to a piano bench and not let him eat or drink or go to the bathroom until he played, and even then he would refuse. Think how bad they would feel when he shriveled up and died of thirst while chained to the piano bench.

They didn't cave in to the melodramatic vow, but in the long run, they couldn't force him to play, so he won. The compromise was that he played only for them and only at home.

Although he would never admit it, he enjoyed these private recitals. Secretly he loved the music that was conducted from his brain to his fingers effortlessly, mindlessly, without any urging from him.

At thirty-eight he still couldn't read a note. Sheet music looked like so many lines and squiggles to him. But over the years, he had honed and refined his innate talent, which remained his secret.

Whenever an acquaintance asked about the piano in his living room, he said it was a legacy from his grandmother, which was true.

He played in order to lose himself in the music. He played for his personal enjoyment or whenever he needed to zone out, empty his mind of the mundane, and allow it to unravel a knotty problem.

Like tonight. There hadn't been a peep out of Savich since the severed tongue incident. The lab at the Georgia Bureau of Investigation had confirmed that it had indeed belonged to Freddy Morris, but that left them no closer to pinning his murder on Savich.

Savich was free. He was free to continue his lucrative drug trafficking, free to kill anyone who crossed him. And Duncan knew that somewhere on Savich's agenda, he was an annotation. Probably his name had a large asterisk beside it.

He tried not to dwell on it. He had other cases, other responsibilities, but it gnawed at him constantly that Savich was out there, biding his time, waiting for the right moment to strike. These days Duncan exercised a bit more caution, was a fraction more vigilant, never went anywhere unarmed. But it wasn't really fear he felt. More like anticipation.

On this night, that supercharged feeling of expectation was keeping him awake. He'd sought refuge from the restlessness by playing his piano. In the darkness of his living room, he was tinkering with a tune of his own composition when his telephone rang.

He glanced at the clock. Work. Nobody called at 1:34 in the morning to report that there *hadn't* been a killing. He answered on the second ring. "Yeah?"

Early in their partnership, he and DeeDee had made a deal. She would be the first one called if they were needed at the scene of a homicide. Between the two of them, he was the one more likely to sleep through a ringing telephone. She was the caffeine junkie and a light sleeper by nature.

He expected the caller to be her and it was. "Were you asleep?" she asked cheerfully.

"Sort of."

"Playing the piano?"

"I don't play the piano."

"Right. Well, stop whatever it is you're doing. We're on."

"Who iced whom?"

"You won't believe it. Pick me up in ten."

"Where—" But he was talking to air. She'd hung up.

He went upstairs, dressed, and slipped on his holster. Within two minutes of his partner's call, he was in his car.

He lived in a town house in the historic district of downtown, only blocks from the police station—the venerable redbrick building known to everyone in Savannah as "the Barracks."

At this hour, the narrow, tree-shrouded streets were deserted. He eased through a couple of red lights on his way out Abercorn Street. DeeDee lived on a side street off that main thoroughfare in a neat duplex with a tidy patch of yard. She was pacing it when he pulled up to the curb.

She got in quickly and buckled her seat belt. Then she cupped her armpits in turn. "I'm already sweating like a hoss. How can it be this hot and sticky at this time of night?"

"Lots of things are hot and sticky at this time of night."

"You've been hanging around with Worley too much."

He grinned. "Where to?"

"Get back on Abercorn."

"What's on the menu tonight?"

"A shooting."

"Convenience store?"

"Brace yourself." She took a deep breath and expelled it. "The home of Judge Cato Laird."

Duncan whipped his head toward her, and only then remembered to brake. The car came to an abrupt halt, pitching them both forward before their seat belts restrained them.

"That's the sum total of what I know," she said in response to his incredulity. "I swear. Somebody at the Laird house was shot and killed."

"Did they say—"

"No. I don't know who."

Facing forward again, he dragged his hand down his face, then took his foot off the brake and applied it heavily to the accelerator. Tires screeched, rubber burned as he sped along the empty streets.

It had been two weeks since the awards dinner, but in quiet moments, and sometimes even during hectic ones, he would experience a flashback to his encounter with Elise Laird. Brief as it had been, tipsy as he'd been, he recalled it vividly: the features of her face, the scent of her perfume, the catch in her throat when he'd said what he had. What a jerk. She was a beautiful woman who had done nothing to deserve the insult. To think she might be dead . . .

He cleared his throat. "I don't know where I'm going."

"Ardsley Park. Washington Street." DeeDee gave him the address. "Very ritzy."

He nodded.

"You okay, Duncan?"

"Why wouldn't I be?"

"I mean, do you feel funny about this?"

"Funny?"

"Come on," she said with asperity. "The judge isn't one of your favorite people."

"Doesn't mean I hope he's dead."

"I know that. I'm just saying."

He shot her a hard look. "Saying *what?*"

"See? That's what I'm talking about. You overreact every time his name comes up. He's a raw nerve with you."

"He gave Savich a free pass and put me in jail."

"And you made an ass of yourself with his wife," she said, matching his tone. "You still haven't told me what you said to her. Was it that bad?"

"What makes you think I said something bad?"

"Because otherwise you would have told me."

He took a corner too fast, ran a stop sign.

"Look, Duncan, if you can't treat this like any other investigation, I need to know."

"It *is* any other investigation."

But when he turned onto Washington and saw in the next block the emergency vehicles, his mouth went dry. The street was divided by a wide median of sprawling oak trees and camellia and azalea bushes. On both sides were stately homes built decades earlier by old money.

He honked his way through the pajama-clad neighbors clustered in the street, and leaned on the horn to move a video cameraman and a reporter who were setting up their shot of the immaculately maintained lawn and the impressive Colonial house with the four fluted columns supporting the second-story balcony. People out for a Sunday drive might slow down to admire the home. Now it was the scene of a fatal shooting.

"How'd the television vans get here so fast? They always beat us," DeeDee complained.

Duncan brought his car to a stop beside the ambulance and got out. Immediately he was assailed with questions from onlookers and reporters. Turning a deaf ear to them, he started toward the house. "You got gloves?" he asked DeeDee over his shoulder. "I forgot gloves."

"You always do. I've got spares."

DeeDee had to take two steps for every one of his as he strode up the front walkway, lined on both sides with carefully tended beds of begonias. Crime scene tape had already been placed around the house. The beat cop at the door recognized them and lifted the tape high enough for them to duck under. "Inside to the left," he said.

"Don't let anyone set foot on the lawn," Duncan instructed the officer. "In fact, keep everybody on the other side of the median."

"Another unit is on the way to help contain the area."

"Good. Forensics?"

"Got here quick."

"Who called the press?"

The cop shrugged in reply.

Duncan entered the massive foyer. The floor was white marble with tiny black squares placed here and there. A staircase hugged a curving wall up to the second floor. Overhead was a crystal chandelier turned up full. There was an enormous arrangement of fresh flowers on a table with carved gilded legs that matched the tall mirror above it.

"Niiiiice," DeeDee said under her breath.

Another uniformed policeman greeted them by name, then motioned with his head toward a wide arched opening to the left. They entered what appeared to be the formal living room. The fireplace was pink marble. Above the mantel was an ugly oil still life of a bowl of fresh vegetables and a dead rabbit. A long sofa with a half dozen fringed pillows faced a pair of matching chairs. Between them was another table with gold legs. A pastel carpet covered the polished hardwood floor, and all of it was lighted by a second chandelier.

Judge Laird, his back to them, was sitting in one of the chairs.

Realizing the logical implication of seeing the judge alive, Duncan felt his stomach drop.

The judge's elbows were braced on his knees, his head down. He was speaking softly to a cop named Crofton, who was balanced tentatively on the edge of the sofa cushion, as though afraid he might get it dirty.

"Elise went downstairs, but that wasn't unusual," Duncan heard the judge say in a voice that was ragged with emotion. He glanced up at the policeman and added, "Chronic insomnia."

Crofton looked sympathetic. "What time was this? That she went downstairs."

"I woke up, partially, when she left the bed. Out of habit, I glanced at the clock on the night table. It was twelve thirty-something. I think." He rubbed his forehead. "I think that's right. Anyway, I dozed off again. The . . . the shots woke me up."

He was saying that someone other than he had shot and killed his wife. Who else was in this house tonight? Duncan wondered.

"I raced downstairs," he continued. "Ran from room to room. I was . . . frantic, a madman. I called her name. Over and over. When I got to the study . . ." His head dropped forward again. "I saw her there, slumped behind the desk."

Duncan felt as though a fist had closed around his throat. He was finding it hard to breathe.

DeeDee nudged him. "Dothan's here."

Dr. Dothan Brooks, medical examiner for Chatham County, was a fat man and made no apology for it. He knew better than anyone that fatty foods could kill you, but he defiantly ate the worst diet possible. He said that he'd seen far worse ways to die than complications from obesity. Considering the horrific manners of death he'd seen over the course of his own career, Duncan thought he might have a point.

As the ME approached them, he removed the latex gloves from

his hands and used a large white handkerchief to mop his sweating forehead, which had taken on the hue of a raw steak. "Detectives." He always sounded out of breath and probably was.

"You beat us here," DeeDee said.

"I don't live far." Looking around, he added with a trace of bitterness, "Definitely at the poorer edge of the neighborhood. This is some place, huh?"

"What have we got?"

"A thirty-eight straight through the heart. Frontal entry. Exit wound in the back. Death was instantaneous. Lots of blood, but, as shootings go, it was fairly neat."

To cover his discomposure, Duncan took the pair of latex gloves DeeDee passed him.

"Can we have a look-see?" she asked.

Brooks stepped aside and motioned them toward the end of the long foyer. "In the study." As they walked, he glanced overhead. "I could send one of my kids to an Ivy League college for what that chandelier cost."

"Who else has been in there?" DeeDee asked.

"The judge. First cops on the scene. Swore they didn't touch anything. I waited on your crime scene boys, didn't go in till they gave me the go-ahead. They're still in there, gathering trace evidence and trying to get a name off the guy."

"*Guy?*" Duncan stopped in his tracks. "The shooter is in custody?"

Dothan Brooks turned and looked at the two of them with perplexity. "Hasn't anybody told y'all what happened here?"

"Obviously not," DeeDee replied.

"The dead man in the study was an intruder," he said. "Mrs. Laird shot him. She's your shooter."

Movement at the top of the staircase drew their gazes upward. Elise Laird was making her way down the stairs followed by a policewoman in uniform. Sally Beale was as black as ebony and hard as steel. Her twin brother was a defensive lineman for the Green Bay Packers. Sally's size alone made her physically imposing. It was coupled with a stern demeanor.

But Duncan's gaze was fixed on Elise Laird. Her face looked

freshly scrubbed. Her pallor couldn't be attributed to the glare of the gaudy chandelier, because even her lips appeared bloodless. Her features were composed, however, and her eyes were dry.

She had killed a man, but she hadn't cried over it.

Her hair was secured with a rubber band at the back of her head. The ponytail looked mercilessly tight. She wore pink suede moccasins on her feet and was dressed in a pair of soft, worn blue jeans and a white sweater that looked like cashmere. With the outdoor temperature hovering around ninety degrees, the sweater seemed out of season. Duncan wondered if she felt chilled, and why.

When she saw Duncan, she halted so suddenly that Officer Beale nearly ran into her. The pause was short-lived, but lasted long enough to be noticed by DeeDee, who gave him a sharp glance.

When Elise reached the bottom step, her gaze locked with Duncan's for several beats before it slid to DeeDee, who stepped forward and introduced herself. "Mrs. Laird, I'm Detective DeeDee Bowen. This is my partner, Detective Sergeant Duncan Hatcher. I think you two have met."

"Darling, did the shower make you feel better?" The judge came from the living room and quickly moved to his wife, placing his arm around her shoulders, touching her colorless cheek with the back of his finger. Only then did he acknowledge the rest of them. Without so much as a hello, he said, addressing the question to Duncan, "Why did they send you?"

"You've got a dead man in your house."

"But you investigate homicides. This wasn't a homicide, Detective Hatcher. My wife shot an intruder, whom she caught in the act of burglarizing my study, where I keep valuable collectibles. When she challenged him, he fired a pistol at her. She had no choice but to protect her own life."

Standard operating procedure was to keep the witnesses of a crime separate until each had been questioned, so that one couldn't influence the other's account in any way. A criminal court judge should know that.

With consternation, Duncan said, "Thanks for the summary, Judge, but we would prefer to hear what happened directly from Mrs. Laird."

"She's already given an account to these officers." He nodded toward Beale and Crofton.

"I talked to her first," Crofton said. "It's pretty much like he said."

"That's her story," Beale confirmed, slapping her notebook against her palm. "His, too."

The judge took umbrage. "It's not a *story*. It's a true account of what took place. Is it necessary for Elise to repeat it tonight? She's already been traumatized."

"We haven't even seen the victim or the scene yet," DeeDee said.

"Once we've taken a look and talked to forensics, we're certain to have questions for Mrs. Laird." Duncan glanced at her. She'd yet to utter a sound. Her eyes were fixed on a spot in near space, as though she had detached herself from what was going on around her.

Coming back to the judge, he said, "We'll try and keep it as brief as possible. We certainly wouldn't want to contribute to the trauma Mrs. Laird has suffered tonight." He turned and addressed Sally Beale. "Why don't you take her into the kitchen? Maybe get her something to drink. Crofton, you can continue with the judge."

Judge Laird didn't look happy about Duncan's directives, which purposefully kept him separated from his missus, but he consented with a terse nod. Stroking his wife's arm, he said, "I'll be in the living room if you need me."

Sally Beale laid her wide hand on Elise's shoulders, firmly but not unkindly. "I could use a Coke or something. How 'bout you?"

Still saying nothing, Elise went along with the policewoman. DeeDee gave Duncan a questioning look. He raised his shoulders in a shrug and proceeded down the hallway to rejoin the ME. "What about it, Dothan? Does it look like self-defense to you?"

"See for yourself."

Duncan and DeeDee paused on the threshold of the study. From that vantage point, they could see only the victim's shoes. They asked the crime scene techs if it was all right to come in.

"Hey, Dunk. DeeDee." Overseeing the collection of evidence was a small, bookish guy named Baker, who looked more like an antiques dealer than a cop who performed the nasty job of scavenging through the rubble of violent death. "We've vacuumed the whole room, but I don't think he got any farther than where you see him now. He jimmied a window lock to break in." He motioned toward the window.

"We found a tire iron outside under the bushes. We've got casts of the footprints outside the window. Matching prints here inside don't extend past the desk. They were muddy prints, so now they're sorta smeared."

"Why's that?"

"The Lairds smeared them when they checked to see was he dead."

"Lairds plural?" DeeDee asked.

Baker nodded. "Her, soon as she shot the guy. The judge when he came into the room and saw what had happened. He assessed the situation and immediately called 911. That's what they told Crofton and Beale anyway."

"Huh. How'd the intruder get here? To the house, I mean."

"Beats me," Baker replied. "We've lifted prints off the desk drawers, but they could belong to the judge, his wife, the housekeeper. We'll see. Took a Ruger nine-millimeter out of his right hand." He held up an evidence bag. "His finger was around the trigger. We're pretty sure he fired. Smelled like it."

"I bagged his hands," Dothan Brooks said.

"We pulled a slug out of the wall over there." Duncan and DeeDee turned to look at where Baker was pointing and saw a bullet hole in the wall about nine feet above the floor.

"If he was trying to shoot Mrs. Laird, his aim was lousy," DeeDee remarked, echoing what Duncan was thinking.

"Maybe she startled him, caught him in the act, and he fired too quickly to take aim," Duncan said.

"That's what we figured," Baker said. He motioned toward the photographer, who was replacing his gear in its hard-shell case. "We got pictures from every angle. I made sketches of the room, and took measurements. It'll all be ready when you need it, if you need it. We're done."

With that, he and his crew trailed out.

Duncan advanced into the room. The victim was lying on the floor, faceup, between a desk that was larger than Duncan's car and a bookcase filled with leather-bound books and knickknacks that looked rare, old, and expensive. The rug beneath him was still wet with blood.

The man was Caucasian, appeared to be around thirty-five, and looked almost embarrassed to be in his present situation. Duncan had been taught by his parents to respect the nobility of life, even in its most ignoble forms. Often his father had reminded him that all men were God's creation, and he'd grown up believing it.

He had acquired enough toughness and objectivity to do the work he did. But he never looked at a dead body without feeling a twinge of sadness. The day he no longer felt it, he would quit. If the time ever came when he felt no remorse over a life taken, he would know his soul was in jeopardy. He would have become one of the lost. He would have become Savich.

He felt he should apologize to this unnamed person for the indignity he had undergone already and would continue to be subjected to until they got from him all the answers he could provide. No longer a person, he was a corpse, evidence, exhibit A.

Duncan knelt down and studied his face, asking softly, "What's your name?"

"Neither the judge nor Mrs. Laird claim to recognize him," Dothan said.

The ME's statement jerked Duncan out of his introspection and back into the job at hand. " 'Claim'?"

"Don't read anything into that. I'm just repeating what the judge told me when I got here."

Duncan and DeeDee exchanged a significant look, then he searched the dead man's pockets, hoping to find something that perhaps Baker had overlooked. All the pockets were empty.

"No car keys. No money. No ID." He studied the man's face again, searching his memory, trying to place him among crooks he'd come across during the investigations of other homicides. "I don't recognize him."

"Me, neither," DeeDee said.

Standing, Duncan said, "Dothan, I'd like to know the distance from which the fatal shot was fired. How close was Mrs. Laird when she shot him?"

"I'll give you my best guess."

"Which is usually pretty damn good."

"Baker's reliable, but I'll take my own measurement of the distance between the door and the desk," DeeDee said, pulling a tape measure from her pocket.

"Well, unless y'all need me, I'm off," the ME said, tucking his damp handkerchief into his pants pocket. "Ready to get him out of here?"

"DeeDee?" Duncan asked.

"Sixteen feet." She wrote the measurement in her notebook, then took a look around the room. "I think I'll do my own sketch of the room, too, but you don't have to hang around," she said to the ME.

"Then I'll send in the EMTs." He glanced around, his expression turning sour. "Money sure gets you nice stuff, doesn't it?"

"Especially old money. Laird Shipping was started by the judge's grandfather, and he's the last of the line," DeeDee informed them. "No other heirs," she said, raising her eyebrows.

"This place probably isn't even mortgaged," Dothan grumbled as he turned to leave. "Think I'll find a Taco Bell open this time of night?" He was panting hard as he lumbered off.

As DeeDee sketched in her notebook, she said, "He's going to keel over one of these days."

"But he'll die happy."

Duncan's mind wasn't on the ME's health. He was noting that the victim's clothing and shoes appeared new, but cheap. The kind a con would wear when he was released from prison. "First thing tomorrow, we need to check men recently released from prison, especially those who'd been serving time for breaking and entering. I bet we won't have to dig too deep before we find this guy."

EMTs wheeled in a gurney. Duncan stood by as the unidentified dead man's body was zipped into the black bag, placed on the gurney, and rolled out. He accompanied it as far as the front door. From there he could see that a larger crowd of gawkers had gathered on the far side of the median. More news vans were parked along the street.

The flowers in the vase on the foyer table shimmied, alerting him to Sally Beale's approach. "I had her go through it all again," she said to Duncan, speaking in an undertone. "Didn't falter. Didn't change a word. She's ready to sign a statement."

He surveyed the divided street, trying to imagine it prior to becoming a crime scene. Without the flashing emergency lights and the onlookers, it would be serene.

"Sally, you were first on the scene, right?"

"Me and Crofton were only a couple blocks away when we got the call from dispatch."

"Did you see any moving vehicles in the area?"

"Nary a one."

"Abandoned car?"

"Not even a moped, and other patrol units have been canvassing the whole neighborhood looking for the perp's means of transportation. Nothing's turned up."

Puzzling. Something out of whack that demanded an explanation. "Are the neighbors being canvassed?"

"Two teams are going door-to-door. So far, everybody was fast asleep, saw no one, heard nothing."

"Not even the shots?" He turned to face the policewoman, who was shrugging.

"Big houses, big yards."

"Mrs. Laird showered?"

"Said she felt violated," Beale said. "Asked would it be okay."

It was a typical reaction for people to want to wash after their home was invaded, but Duncan didn't like it when a bloody corpse was just downstairs. "Did she have blood on her?"

"No, and I was with her the whole time upstairs. All she had on was her robe. I got it from her, gave it to Baker. No blood on it that I saw. But the judge, the hem of his robe had blood on it from when he checked the body. He asked permission to dress. Baker's got his robe, too."

"Okay, thanks, Sally. Keep them separate till we're ready to question them."

"You got it."

He returned to the study, where DeeDee was examining the judge's desk. "All these drawers are still locked."

"Mrs. Laird must have caught the burglar early."

She raised her head and gave him an arch look. "You believe the burglar scenario?"

"I believe it's time we asked just how this went down."

CHAPTER

4

"WHO FIRST, HER OR THE JUDGE?"

Duncan thought about it. "Let's talk to them together."

DeeDee registered surprise as well as a trace of disapproval. "How come?"

"Because they've already been questioned separately by Crofton and Beale. Sally Beale told me Mrs. Laird's second telling didn't vary from the first and that she's prepared to sign a statement.

"If it really is a matter of her shooting a home intruder, and we continue badgering them, it's going to look like we doubt them, and *that* will seem like reprisal for my contempt charge. The only thing it will accomplish is to piss off the judge. Gerard will have my ass if I have another run-in with him."

"Okay," DeeDee said. "But what if it isn't a case of her protecting herself from a home intruder?"

"We have no reason to disbelieve them, do we?"

He left DeeDee to mull that over and followed his nose until he located the kitchen, where Sally Beale and Elise Laird were seated at the table in the breakfast nook, talking quietly. When he came in, the policewoman, in the manner of a heavy person, pushed herself to her feet. "We're finished here." She closed the cover of her spiral notebook. "I've got it all down."

None of the color had returned to Elise Laird's face. She looked at him inquisitively. He sensed unspoken apprehension.

"We're ready for you in the living room, Mrs. Laird."

He made his way back to the formal room, where Crofton and Judge Laird had been joined by an austere, gray-haired woman who was pouring hot liquid from a silver pot into china cups.

Sally Beale, who had escorted Elise Laird from the kitchen, came up behind Duncan and noticed his curiosity. "The housekeeper," she said in a low rumble. "Something Berry. Blew into the kitchen twenty minutes ago like she owned the place." She chuckled. "'Bout keeled over when she saw my big black self sitting at the breakfast table."

"So she doesn't live in?"

She shook her head. "Apparently the judge called her to duty and she came running in no time flat. She's prepared to do battle for him."

From over his shoulder, Duncan gave the policewoman a significant look. "For him, but not for Mrs. Laird?"

"All the time she was boiling water and preparing the tea tray, she didn't say boo to the lady of the house. You couldn't melt an ice cube on that one's ass." She raised her shoulders in an indolent shrug. "I call 'em as I see 'em."

The judge stood up and warmly embraced his wife when she rejoined him. They were talking together softly, but Crofton was close enough to overhear, so Duncan reasoned that Judge Laird was only asking his wife how she was faring.

Crofton, trying to balance the dainty teacup and saucer on his knee while jotting something in his notebook, greeted Duncan and DeeDee's appearance with evident relief. "I'll turn it over to the detectives now." He set the china on the nearest table, then left the room along with Beale.

Duncan and DeeDee took the twin chairs facing the sofa, where the judge and his wife sat shoulder to shoulder, thigh to thigh. Neither had touched the steaming cups of tea in front of them. Laird offered some to Duncan and DeeDee.

Duncan declined. DeeDee smiled up at the sour-faced housekeeper. "Do you have a Diet Coke?"

She left the room to fetch the drink.

"Have they removed it?"

Duncan supposed the judge was referring to the corpse. "Yes. On his way to the morgue."

"Where he belongs," he muttered with distaste.

Elise Laird tipped her head down. Duncan noticed her hands were tightly clasped together and that she had pulled the sleeves of her sweater down over the backs of them as though to keep them warm.

The housekeeper returned with DeeDee's Diet Coke, served over ice in a crystal tumbler on a small plate with a doily and a lacy cloth napkin. To her credit, and Duncan's surprise, DeeDee thanked the housekeeper graciously. Any other time, she would have been breaking up with laughter, or scorn, over such pretentious finery.

At a motion from the judge, Mrs. Berry withdrew, leaving the four of them alone. The judge placed his arm around his wife and drew her closer to him. He looked at her with concern, then focused on Duncan.

"We've told the other officers everything we know. They took copious notes. I don't know what more we could possibly add, although we want to do everything we can to resolve this issue as quickly as possible." His expression was earnest, concerned.

"I hate asking you to retell what happened, but Detective Bowen and I need to hear it all for ourselves," Duncan said. "I'm sure you understand."

"Of course. Let's just get it over with so I can take Mrs. Laird to bed."

"I'll make it as painless as possible," Duncan said, flashing his most reassuring grin. "However, during our questioning, Judge, I'll ask you not to offer a comment or answer unless directly asked. Please say nothing that could influence Mrs. Laird's recollection. It's important that we hear—"

"I understand the procedure, Detective." Although the judge's interruption was rude and his tone brusque, his expression remained as pleasant as Duncan's. "Please proceed."

The man's condescending tone grated on Duncan. The judge was accustomed to running the show. In his courtroom, he was the despotic authority. But this was Duncan's arena and he was the ring-master. Lest his anger get him into trouble, Duncan thought it best to let DeeDee begin, ease them into it. He'd take over when it got down to the nitty-gritty.

He gave DeeDee a subtle nod and she picked up the cue immedi-ately. "Mrs. Laird?" DeeDee waited until Elise raised her head and looked at her. "Can you lead us through what happened here to-night?"

Before beginning, Elise took a deep breath. "I came downstairs to get something to drink."

"She does nearly every night," the judge chimed in, flouting Duncan's request that he not speak until asked.

Duncan chose to let it pass. Once. "You suffer from chronic in-somnia," he said, remembering what he'd heard the judge tell Crofton.

"Yes." She addressed the reply to DeeDee, not to him. "I was on my way to the kitchen when—"

"Excuse me. What time was this?" DeeDee asked.

"Around twelve thirty. I remember looking at the clock shortly after midnight. It was about half an hour later that I got up and came downstairs. I thought a glass of milk would help me fall asleep. Sometimes it does."

She paused, as though expecting someone to comment on that. When no one did, she continued. "I was in the kitchen when I heard a noise."

"What kind of noise?"

She turned toward Duncan, meeting his eyes for the first time since that moment in the kitchen. "I wasn't sure what I heard. I'm still not. I think maybe it was his footfalls. Or him bumping into a piece of furniture. Something like that."

"Okay."

"Whatever it was, I knew the sound was coming from the study."

"You couldn't identify the noise, but you knew where it was coming from?"

The judge frowned at the skepticism underlying DeeDee's ques-tion, but he didn't say anything.

"I know that sounds odd," Elise said.

"It does."

"I'm sorry." She raised her hands palms up. "That's how it was."

"I don't see why this couldn't wait until tomorrow morning," the judge said.

Before Duncan could admonish him, Elise said, "No, Cato. I'd rather talk about it now. While it's still fresh in my mind."

He studied his wife's face, saw the determination in her expression, and sighed. "If you're sure you're up to it." She nodded. He kissed her brow, then divided an impatient look between DeeDee and Duncan, ending on him. "She heard a noise, realized where it was coming from, thought—as any rational person would—that we had an intruder."

Duncan looked at Elise. "Is that what you thought?"

"Yes. I immediately thought that someone was inside the house."

"You have an alarm system."

Duncan had noted the keypad on the wall of the foyer just inside the front door. He'd seen a motion detector in the study and assumed that similar detectors were in other rooms as well. Homes of this caliber almost always had sophisticated alarm systems. A judge who'd sent countless miscreants to prison would surely want his home protected against any ex-con with a vendetta in mind.

"We have a state-of-the-art monitored security system," the judge said.

"It wasn't set?" Duncan asked.

"Not tonight," the judge replied.

"Why not?" The judge was about to answer. Duncan held up his hand, indicating he wanted to hear the answer from Elise. "Mrs. Laird?"

"I . . ." She faltered, cleared her throat, then said more assertively, "I failed to set the alarm tonight."

"Are you usually the one who sets it?"

"Yes. Every night. Routinely."

"But tonight you forgot." DeeDee put it in the form of a statement, but she was really asking how Mrs. Laird could forget to do tonight what was her routine to do every night.

"I didn't exactly forget."

These questions about the alarm had made her uneasy. An uneasy witness was a witness who was either withholding information or downright lying. An uneasy witness was one you prodded. "If you didn't forget, why wasn't the alarm set?" Duncan asked.

She opened her mouth to speak. But no words came out.

"Why wasn't it set, Mrs. Laird?" he repeated.

"Oh, for crissake," the judge muttered. "I'm forced to be indelicate, but seeing as we're all adults—"

"Judge, please—"

"No, Detective Hatcher. Since my wife is too embarrassed to answer your question, I'll answer for her. Earlier tonight we enjoyed a bottle of wine together in our Jacuzzi. From there we went to bed and made love. Afterward, Elise was . . . Let's just say she was *disinclined* to leave the bed in order to set the alarm."

The judge paused for effect. The air in the room suddenly became abnormally still. Hot. Dense. Or so it seemed to Duncan. He became aware of his pulse. His scalp felt tight.

Finally the judge ended the taut silence. "Now, can we move beyond this one point and talk about the man who tried to kill Elise?"

An inactivated alarm system was a significant point in the investigation of a home break-in that had resulted in a fatal shooting. As the lead detective conducting the investigation, that's what Duncan should have been concentrating on.

But instead, he was having a hard time getting past the idea of a bottle of wine and Elise Laird in a tub of bubbles. To say nothing of an Elise Laird in bed, sexually sated to the point of immobility.

And when an erotic visualization of that flashed into his mind, it wasn't Cato Laird who was lying with her.

As though reading his mind, DeeDee shot him a look of reproof, then addressed the next question to Mrs. Laird. "When you heard the noise, what did you do?"

As though grateful for the new direction of questioning, she turned to DeeDee. "I went through the butler's pantry, which is the shortest route from the kitchen into the foyer. When I reached the foyer, I was certain there was someone in the study."

"What made you certain?" DeeDee asked.

She raised her slender shoulders. "Instinct. I sensed his presence."

"*His* presence? You knew it was a man? Instinctually?"

Elise's gaze swung back to Duncan. "I assumed so, Detective Hatcher." She continued to look at him for a moment, then turned back to DeeDee. "I was afraid. It was dark. I sensed someone inside the house. I . . . I took a pistol from the drawer in the hall table."

"Why didn't you run to the nearest telephone, dial 911?"

"I wish I had. If I had it to do over—"

"You would be the one on the way to the morgue." Cato Laird took one of her hands and pressed it between his. He kissed her temple near her hairline.

Duncan interrupted the tender exchange. "You knew there was a pistol in that drawer?"

"Yes," she replied.

"Had you used it before?"

She looked affronted. "Of course not."

"Then how did you know it was there?"

"I own several guns, Detective," the judge said. "They're kept handy. Elise knows where they are. I made sure of that. I also insisted on her taking lessons to learn how to use the guns to protect herself in the event she should need to."

She learned well, Duncan thought. She'd shot a man straight through the heart. He was a good marksman, but he doubted he could be that accurate under duress.

To defuse another tense moment, DeeDee prompted Elise. "So you have the pistol."

"I walked toward the study. When I got to the door, I switched on the light. But I flipped the wrong switch and the light in the foyer came on, not the overhead light in the study. They're on the same switch plate. Anyway, I illuminated myself, not him, but I could see him, standing there behind the desk."

"What did he do?"

"Nothing. He just stood there, frozen, looking startled, staring at me. I said, 'Get out of here. Go away.' But he didn't move."

"Did he say anything?"

She held Duncan's gaze for several seconds, then replied with a terse no.

He was absolutely certain she was lying. Why? he wondered. But he decided not to challenge her about it now. "Go on."

"Suddenly he jerked his arm up. Like a puppet whose string has been yanked. His hand came up and before it even registered with me that he had a gun, he fired it. I . . . I reacted instantaneously."

"You fired back."

She nodded.

No one spoke for a time. Finally DeeDee said, "Your aim was exceptionally good, Mrs. Laird."

"Thank God," the judge said.

More quietly Elise said, "I got lucky."

Neither Duncan nor DeeDee said anything to that, although DeeDee glanced at him to see if he thought that shot could be attributed to luck.

"What happened next, Mrs. Laird?"

"I checked his body for a pulse."

Duncan remembered Baker saying that the victim's muddy footprints had been smeared, probably by both the Lairds.

"He fell backward, out of sight," she said. "I was terrified, afraid that he was . . ."

"Still alive?" DeeDee said.

Again Elise appeared to take umbrage. "No, Detective Bowen," she said testily. "I was afraid that he was *dead*. When I got up this morning, I didn't plan on ending a man's life tonight."

"I didn't imply that you had."

The judge said brusquely, "That's it, detectives. No more questions. She's told you what you need to know. The law is clear on what constitutes self-defense. This intruder was inside our home, and he posed an imminent threat to Elise's life. If he had survived, you'd be charging him with a list of felonies, including assault with a deadly weapon. Shooting him was justified, and I believe my wife is being inordinately generous by wishing he had survived."

Duncan leveled a hard look on him. "I remind you again, Judge, that this is my investigation. Think of it as my equivalent to your courtroom. I've extended you the courtesy of being present while I question Mrs. Laird, but if you insist on contributing another word without being asked to, you'll be excused and I'll conduct the interview with her alone."

The judge's jaw turned rigid and his eyes glittered with resentment, but he gave a negligent wave of his hand. It wasn't a gesture of concession. He made it appear he was granting Duncan permission to continue.

Duncan turned his attention back to Elise. "You felt for a pulse?"

She pulled her hand from her husband's grasp, crossed her arms over her chest, and hugged herself. "I didn't want to touch him. But I forced myself. I went into the room—"

"Did you still have the pistol?"

"I had dropped it. It was on the floor, there at the door."

"Okay," Duncan said.

"I went into the study and stepped around the desk. I knelt down, put my fingers here."

She touched her own throat approximately where her carotid would be. Duncan noticed that her fingers were very slender. They looked bloodless, cold. Whereas the skin of her throat . . .

He yanked his eyes away from her neck and looked at the judge. "I overheard you telling Officer Crofton that when you reached the study, you found Elise slumped behind the desk."

"That's correct. She was slumped in the desk chair. I thought . . . well, you can't imagine the fear that gripped me. I thought she was dead. I rushed over to her. That's when I saw the man on the floor. I'm not ashamed of the relief I felt at that moment."

"You had blood on your robe."

He shuddered with revulsion. "There was already a lot of blood on the carpet beneath him. My hem dipped into it when I bent over the body. I felt for a pulse. There wasn't one."

"What were you doing at this point?"

If DeeDee hadn't asked that of Elise, Duncan would have. He'd been watching her out the corner of his eye. She'd been listening raptly to her husband's account. If he'd said anything contradictory to what she'd experienced, she hadn't shown it.

"I was . . . I wasn't doing anything. Just sitting there in the chair. I was numb."

Too numb to cry. He remembered her eyes being dry, with no sign of weeping. She hadn't shed a tear, but at least she hadn't lied about it.

The judge said, "Elise was in shock. I probably remember more at this point than she does. May I speak?"

Duncan realized he was being patronized, but he let it pass. "Please, Judge," he said with exaggerated politeness.

"I picked Elise out of the chair and carried her from the room. I stepped over the pistol, which was on the floor just inside the study door, as she said. I left it there and didn't touch the body again or anything else in the room. I deposited Elise here in the living room and used that telephone to call 911." He pointed out a cordless phone on an end table. "No one went into the study until the officers arrived."

"While you were waiting on them, did you ask her what had happened?"

"Of course. She explained in stops and starts, but I got the gist of it. In any case, it was rather obvious that she'd interrupted an attempted burglary."

Not so obvious from where I sit, Judge. Duncan didn't speak his thought aloud because there was no point in riling the judge unnecessarily. However, there were some details that needed further investigation and explanation before he was ready to rubber-stamp this a matter of self-defense and close the books on it. Getting an identity on the dead man would be the first step. That could shed some light on why he was in the Lairds' home study.

Duncan smiled at the couple. "I think that's all we need to go over tonight. There may be some loose ends to clear up tomorrow." He stood up, essentially putting an end to the interview. "Thank you. I know this wasn't easy. I apologize for the need to put you through it."

"You were only doing your job, Detective." The judge extended his hand and Duncan shook it.

"Yes. I was." Releasing the judge's hand, he added, "For the time being, the study is still a crime scene. I'm sorry if this poses an inconvenience, but please don't remove anything from it."

"Of course."

"I have one more question," DeeDee said. "Did either of you recognize the man?"

"I didn't," Elise said.

"Nor I," said the judge.

"You're sure? Because Mrs. Laird said she'd turned on the wrong light. The room would have been semi-dark. Did you turn on the overhead light in the study, Judge?"

"Yes, I did. I explained to Officer Crofton that on my way into the room, I switched on the light."

"So, with the overhead light on, you got a good look at the man?"

"A very good look. As stated, he was a stranger to us, Detective Bowen." He softened the edge in his voice by politely offering to see them out. Before leaving Elise, he bent down to where she had remained seated on the sofa. "I'll be right back, darling, then I'll take you up."

She nodded and gave him a weak smile.

Duncan and DeeDee walked from the room with him. When they reached the foyer, DeeDee said, "Judge, before we leave, I'd like to measure the height of that bullet hole in the wall. It'll only take a sec."

He looked annoyed by the request, but said, "Certainly," and motioned her to follow him toward the study.

Duncan stayed where he was in a deceptively relaxed stance, hands in his pants pockets, staring after his partner and the judge as they moved down the foyer out of earshot.

Beale and Crofton were talking together at the front door. From the snatches of conversation Duncan could overhear, they were discussing the pros and cons of various barbecue joints and ignoring the reporters and curiosity seekers still loitering in the street, waiting for something exciting to happen.

He looked into the living room. Elise was still on the sofa. She had picked up her cup of tea, but left the saucer on the coffee table.

Both her hands were folded around the cup. They looked as delicate as the china. She was staring down into the tea.

Quietly Duncan said, "I was drunk."

She didn't move or show any reaction whatsoever, although he knew she had heard him.

"I was also pissed off at your husband."

Her fingers contracted a little more tightly around the cup.

"Neither excuses what I said to you. But I, uh . . ." He glanced toward both ends of the foyer. Still empty. He was safe to speak. "I want you to know . . . what I said? It wasn't about you."

She raised her head and turned toward him. Her face was still wan, her lips colorless, making her eyes look exceptionally large. Large enough for a man to fall into and become immersed in the green depths of them. "Wasn't it?"

CHAPTER
5

Upon seeing Robert Savich for the first time, people were initially struck by his unusual coloring.

His skin tone was that of café au lait, a legacy from his maternal grandmother, a Jamaican who'd come to the United States seeking a better life. At age thirty-four she had given up the quest by slashing her wrists in a bathtub in the brothel where she lived and worked. Her leached body was discovered by another of the whores, her fifteen-year-old daughter, baby Robert's mother.

His blue eyes had been passed down through generations of Saviches, a disreputable lineage no more promising than his maternal one.

Superficially, he was accepted for what he was. But he knew that neither pure blacks nor pure whites would ever wholly accept his mingled blood and embrace him as one of their own. Prejudice found fertile ground in every race. It recognized no borders. It permeated every society on earth, no matter how vociferously it was denounced.

So from the time he could reason, Savich had understood that he must create a dominion that was solely his. A man didn't achieve an egotistic goal of that caliber by being a nice guy, but rather by being tougher, smarter, meaner than his peers. A man could do it only by evoking fear in anyone he met.

Young Robert had taken the dire experiences of his childhood and youth and turned them to his advantage. Each year of poverty, abuse, and alienation was like an additional application of varnish, which became harder and more protective, until now, he was impenetrable. This was particularly true of his soul.

He had directed his intelligence and entrepreneurial instincts toward commerce—of a sort. He was dealing crack cocaine by the time he was twelve. At age twenty-five, in a coup that included slitting the throat of his mentor in front of awed competitors, he established himself as the lord of a criminal fiefdom. Those who hadn't known his name up to that point soon did. Rivals began showing up dead by gruesome means. His well-earned reputation for ruthlessness rapidly spread, effectively quelling any dreamed-of mutinies.

His reign of terror had continued for a decade. It had made him wealthy beyond even his expectations. Minor rebellions staged by those reckless or stupid enough to cross him were immediately snuffed. Betrayal spelled death to the betrayer.

Ask Freddy Morris. Not that he could answer you.

As Savich wheeled into the parking lot of the warehouse from which he ran his legitimate machine shop, he chuckled yet again, imagining Duncan Hatcher's reaction upon finding the little gift that had been left in his refrigerator.

Duncan Hatcher had started as a pebble in his shoe, nothing more than a nuisance. Initially his crusade to destroy Savich's empire had been somewhat amusing. But Hatcher's determination hadn't waned. Each defeat seemed only to strengthen his resolve. Savich was no longer amused. The detective had become an increasingly dangerous threat who must be dealt with. Soon.

The gradual introduction of methamphetamine into the Southeastern states had opened up a new and vigorous market. It was an ever-expanding profit center for Savich's business. But it was a demanding taskmaster, requiring constant vigilance. He had his hands full controlling those who manufactured and marketed meth for him. He was equally busy keeping independents from poaching on his territory.

Any idiot with a box of cold remedy and a can of fuel thought he could go into business for himself. Fortunately, most of the amateurs blew themselves and their makeshift labs to smithereens without any help from him. But as relatively easy as it was to produce, meth was even easier to market. Because of its various forms of ingestion—snorting, smoking, injecting, and simply swallowing—there was something to suit every user.

It was a lucrative trade, and Savich didn't want Duncan Hatcher to bugger it up.

The machine shop on the ground floor of the warehouse was noisy, nasty, and hot, in contrast to the cool oasis of his office suite upstairs. The two areas were separated by a short ride in a clanking service elevator, but aesthetically they were worlds apart.

He'd spared no expense to surround himself with luxury. His leather desk chair was as soft as butter. The finish on his desk was satin smooth and glossy. The carpet was woven of silk threads, the finest money could buy.

His secretary was a homosexual named Kenny, whose family had deep roots in Savannah society and, unfortunately for Kenny, longevity genes. Kenny was waiting impatiently for his elderly parents to die and leave him, their only son and heir, his much-anticipated paper mill fortune.

In the meantime he worked for Savich, who was dark and mysterious and exciting, who was anathema to his stodgy parents for every reason thinkable, and who had won Kenny's undying loyalty by slowly choking to death a violent homophobe who had waylaid Kenny outside a gay bar and beaten him to within an inch of his life.

Their working relationship was mutually beneficial. Savich preferred Kenny to a female secretary. Invariably women got around to wanting a sexual relationship with him, the depth of which depended on the woman. His policy had always been to keep romance and business separate.

Besides, women were too easily swayed by flattery, or even kindness. Cops and federal agents often used this feminine weakness as a means of getting information. They'd once tried that tactic in the hope of incriminating him. It failed when his secretary mysteriously disappeared. She'd never been found. He'd replaced her with Kenny.

Kenny shot to his feet the instant Savich crossed the threshold of the office suite. Although his well-coiffed hair remained well-coiffed as he nodded toward the closed door to Savich's private office, it was apparent that he was in a state of excitability.

"You have a visitor who wouldn't take no for an answer," he said in an exaggerated stage whisper.

Instantly alert to the danger of an ambush—his first thought was *Hatcher*—Savich reached for the pistol at the small of his back.

His secretary's plucked eyebrows arched fearfully. "It's not like *that*. I would have called you if it was like *that*. I believe you'll want to see this visitor."

Savich, now more curious than wary, moved to the door of his private chamber and opened it. His guest was standing with her back to the room, staring out the window. Hearing him, she turned and removed the dark sunglasses that concealed half her face.

"Elise! What an unexpected and delightful surprise. You're always a sight for sore eyes."

She didn't return either his wide smile or his flattery. "I'm glad to hear that because I need a favor."

Duncan's rank as detective sergeant afforded few benefits above those of his colleagues, but one of them was a private office at the back of the narrow room that was home to the Violent Crimes Unit.

Duncan nodded at DeeDee as he walked past her desk. He had a doughnut stuck in his mouth, a Styrofoam cup of coffee in one hand, his sport jacket hooked on a finger of the other, a newspaper tucked under his arm. He stepped into his office, but before he even had a chance to sit down, DeeDee, who'd followed him into the closet-sized office, laid a folder on his desk with a decisive slap.

"His name was Gary Ray Trotter."

Duncan wasn't a morning person. Hated them, in fact. It took a while for him to warm up to the idea of daylight and get all his pistons firing. DeeDee, on the other hand, could go from zero to sixty within a few seconds.

Despite their late night at the Lairds' house, she would have been up and at 'em for hours. Other detectives had straggled into the VCU this morning, looking already sapped by the cloying humidity outside. DeeDee, not surprisingly, was by far the most chipper of the lot and was practically bristling with energy.

Duncan raised his arm and let the newspaper slide onto his desk. He draped his jacket over the back of his chair, set down the coffee, which had grown hot in his hand despite the cardboard sleeve around the cup, and took a bite from the doughnut before removing it from his mouth.

"No 'good morning'?" he asked grumpily.

"Dothan got to work early, too," she told him as he plopped into his desk chair. "He fingerprinted the Lairds' corpse. Gary Ray Trotter was a repeat offender, so I had the ID in a matter of minutes. Lots of stuff on this guy." She indicated the folder lying still untouched on his desk.

"Originally from Baltimore, over the last dozen years he's gradually worked his way down the East Coast, spending time in various jails for petty stuff until a couple of years ago he got brave and expanded into armed robbery in Myrtle Beach. He was released on parole three months ago. His parole officer hadn't heard from him in two."

"My, you've been busy," Duncan said.

"I thought one of us should get a running start, and I knew you wouldn't."

"See, that's why we work so well together. I recognize your strengths."

"Or rather, I recognize your weaknesses."

Smiling over the barb, he flipped open the file folder and scanned the top sheet. "I thought his clothes looked new. Like a con recently out."

By the time he'd finished reading Gary Ray Trotter's rap sheet he had eaten the doughnut. He licked the glaze off his fingers. "He didn't have a very distinguished criminal career," he remarked as he removed the plastic top from the coffee cup.

"Right. So I don't get it."

" 'It'?"

DeeDee pulled a chair closer to Duncan's desk and sat down. "Burglarizing the Lairds' house seems a trifle ambitious for Gary Ray."

Duncan shrugged. "Maybe he wanted to go out with a bang."

"Ha-ha."

"I couldn't resist."

"He'd never been charged with burglary before," DeeDee said.

"Doesn't mean he didn't commit one."

"No, but from reading his record, he doesn't come across as the sharpest knife in the drawer. In fact, his first offense at age sixteen was theft of a bulldozer."

"I thought that was a typo. It really was a bulldozer?"

"He drove it from the road construction site where he was employed as a flagman. You know, orange vest? Waves cars around roadwork?"

"Got it."

"Okay, so Gary Ray steals a bulldozer and drives it to his folks' farmhouse, leaves it parked outside. Next morning, the road crew shows up for work, discovers the bulldozer missing, calls the police, who—"

"Followed the tracks straight to it."

"Duh!" DeeDee exclaimed. "How dumb can you be?"

Duncan laughed. "Where was he going to fence a bulldozer?"

"See what I mean? Our Gary Ray wasn't too astute. It's quite a leap from bulldozer theft to breaking into a house with a sophisticated alarm system. It wasn't set, but Gary Ray didn't know that when he went at that window with a tire iron."

Playing devil's advocate, Duncan said, "He'd had years to perfect his craft."

"Wouldn't that include coming prepared? Bringing along the tools of his trade? Let's say Gary Ray had become a crackerjack burglar. Doubtful, but let's say. One who knew how to disarm sophisticated alarm systems, cut glass so he could reach in and unlock windows, stuff like that."

"Your basic Hollywood-heist type with his fancy techno toys."

"I guess," she said. "So, anyway, where was Gary Ray's gear? All he brought with him was that tire iron."

"And a Ruger nine-millimeter."

"Well, that. But nothing to pick locks or crack safes. Nothing he could use to break into a desk drawer."

"Those locks would be simple, the kind you open with a tiny key.

Give me a few seconds and I could pick them with a safety pin," Duncan said.

"Gary Ray didn't have even that. And another thing, even if you were the dumbest burglar in history, wouldn't you at least wear gloves to avoid leaving fingerprints?"

None of the points she'd raised were revelations to Duncan. When he'd returned home in the wee hours, he'd made an earnest effort to sleep. But his mind was busy with jumbled thoughts about Elise Laird's account of the events that had left a man dead, and about the judge's urgency for them to accept her account without question.

Every discrepancy that DeeDee had cited, he'd already considered. Even before he knew that Gary Ray was an inept criminal, the break-in seemed ill planned and poorly executed. Failure was practically guaranteed.

Nevertheless, he continued to argue the points. "You're assuming that Gary Ray planned this burglary." He tapped the folder. "According to this, he was a drug user. He started life stupid and then cooked his few good brain cells with controlled substances.

"Supposing he's in bad need of a fix, has no money, sees a house that's bound to have good stuff in it, stuff he can grab quick and fence within a half hour. He could get at least one good toot out of a crystal paperweight or silver candlestick."

DeeDee thought it over for several moments, then shook her head. "Maybe I'd buy that scenario if he'd been in a commercial area. He pulls a crash-and-snatch on an electronics store or something. Even if the alarm is blaring, he could be in and out in a matter of seconds with a goodie in his pocket.

"But not out there in the burbs," she went on. "Especially on foot. No one's found a car attached to him. I checked as soon as I got here this morning. What was he doing in that neighborhood without a getaway car?"

"I wondered about that last night," Duncan admitted. "It's been nagging me ever since. How'd he get there and how did he plan to get out?"

"If he didn't have a car, where'd the tire iron come from?" she asked. "Which, when you think about it, is a pretty clumsy apparatus for a burglar."

The high humidity had upped the frizz factor of her hair. It swept the air like a stiff broom when she shook her head again. "No, Duncan, something's out of joint."

"So what do you think?"

She propped her forearms on the edge of his desk and leaned forward. "I don't think we're getting the straight story from the angel-faced Mrs. Laird."

Dammit, that's what he thought, too.

He didn't want to think it. He'd spent the early morning hours trying to convince himself that Elise Laird was as true blue as a nun, had never told a lie in her life, had never even fudged the truth.

But his detective's gut instinct was telling him otherwise. His master's degree was telling him otherwise. Fifteen years of police work was telling him that something didn't gibe, that the judge's hot tub buddy had intentionally left something out or, worse, made it all up.

Obviously his partner questioned Elise's veracity, and DeeDee didn't even know about the private exchange that he'd had with Elise.

He told himself not to read anything into that, that it was irrelevant, and to forget it. However, in addition to sorting through the elements of the shooting incident that didn't add up, his mind frequently wandered back to that moment when a simple, two-word question had become foreplay.

"Wasn't it?"

Each time he thought about it—the husky pitch of her voice, the expression in her eyes—he had a profound physical reaction. Like now.

For a cop, it was a bad and dangerous reaction to have to a woman who'd fatally shot a man. For a cop who'd criticized fellow officers for having similar lapses in judgment and morality, it was hypocritical.

It was also damned inconvenient, when DeeDee was sitting across the desk, watching him, waiting for his assessment of Elise Laird's story.

"What do you know about her?" he asked in a reasonably normal voice. "Her history, I mean."

"How would I know her history? She and I hardly run in the same circles."

"You recognized her the night of the awards dinner."

"From her pictures in the newspaper. If you read something besides the sports page and the crossword puzzle, you would have recognized her, too."

"She's featured frequently?"

"Always looking sensational, wearing haute couture, attached at the hip to the judge. She's definitely a trophy for His Honor."

"Do some digging. See what you can find on her. I'll go over to the morgue, goose Dothan into giving priority to Gary Ray Trotter's autopsy. We'll compare notes when I get back." He drained his coffee cup. Then, trying not to appear self-conscious, he stood up and reached for his sport jacket.

"Duncan?"

"Yeah?"

"I just realized something."

He was afraid DeeDee would say something like, *I just realized that you're sporting a boner for the judge's wife.*

But what she said was, "I just realized that we're not treating this shooting like it was self-defense. We're investigating it as something else, aren't we?"

He almost wished she'd said the other thing.

He called the ME from his car and prevailed upon him to put Gary Ray Trotter at the head of the line. Dr. Dothan Brooks had already opened up the cadaver by the time Duncan arrived.

"So far, all his organs are normal size and weight," Dothan said over his shoulder as he placed a hunk of tissue on the scale.

Duncan took up a position against the wall, listening and watching as the ME methodically went about his work. He glanced at the cadaver only occasionally. He wasn't particularly squeamish. In fact, he was fascinated by the information a cadaver could impart.

But his fascination made him feel guilty. He felt like he was no better than people who rushed to the scene of a tragedy in the perverse hope of glimpsing strewn body parts and blood.

The ME finished and turned the human shell over to his assistant to close. After he had washed up, Dothan joined Duncan, who was waiting for him in his office.

"Cause of death was obvious," he said as he huffed in. "His heart was pulp. Exit wound bigger than a salad plate."

"Before I got here, did you see any other wounds, bruises, scratches?"

"Was he in a fight, you mean? Struggle of some sort?" He shook his head. "Nothing under his fingernails except your common dirt, and there was gunpowder residue on his right hand. He had a broken toe on his left foot, long time ago. No surgical scars. He hadn't been circumcised."

"From how far away would you say he was shot?" Duncan asked.

"Fifteen feet, give or take."

"About the distance between the door of the study and the desk." He remembered that DeeDee had measured it at sixteen feet. "So Mrs. Laird was telling the truth."

"About that." Dothan unwrapped the corned beef sandwich that had been waiting for him on his desk. "Early lunch. Want half?"

"No, thanks. Do you think Mrs. Laird was lying about something else?"

Brooks took a huge bite, but blotted mustard from the corners of his lips with surprising daintiness. He chewed, swallowed, belched, then said, "Possibly. Maybe not. There's the question of who fired first."

"You said Trotter died instantly. Meaning he would have had to shoot first."

"Then you've got to believe he was blind—he wasn't—or the worst marksman in the history of crime."

"Maybe he deliberately aimed high. He was only trying to frighten her with a warning shot."

"Could be," Dothan said, nodding in time to his chewing. "Or maybe she startled him when she appeared in the doorway. Trotter had a knee-jerk reaction, fired a wild shot."

"She didn't startle him. She said she told him to leave. He just stood there, looking at her, then jerked his arm up—that's the word she used—and fired."

"Hmm." The ME talked around a big bite of sandwich. "Then I suppose he was extremely nervous, which would account for his aim being nowhere near her. Another possibility"—he paused to slurp Dr Pepper from a paper cup the size of a small wastebasket—"is that he was in the act of firing when her bullet struck him. His finger reflexively contracted and completed the action that pulled the trigger as he was falling backward." He swallowed. "Now that I think on it, the angle would be right for where the bullet struck the wall."

He acted it out, pretending to fall backward, his index finger serving as the barrel of a pretend pistol. As he went back, his aim moved to a spot high on the wall, far above Duncan's head.

"Could that happen?" Duncan asked. "A reflex like that at the moment your heart is blown to hell?"

Brooks crammed the remainder of his sandwich into his mouth. "I've seen fatal bullet wounds with even more bizarre explanations. You wouldn't believe how far-fetched."

"So what are you telling me?"

"I'm telling you that anything can happen, Detective. But lucky for me, it's your job to find out what actually did."

"I've put them in the sunroom, Mrs. Laird."

"That's fine."

Mrs. Berry had come upstairs to inform her that the same detectives who'd been at the house the night before were downstairs and had asked to see her. "Could you please bring in some refreshments? Diet Coke and iced tea."

The formidable housekeeper nodded. "Shall I tell them you'll be right down?"

"Please."

Elise shut the bedroom door, then stood there, wondering what questions the detectives would be asking today.

Hadn't they believed her last night?

If they had, they wouldn't be back today, would they?

Loose ends, Detective Hatcher had said. The term could cover any number of inconsequential nagging details. Or it could be an understatement for discrepancies of major importance.

She feared the latter.

That's what had prompted her to go see Savich this morning. It had been risky, but she'd wanted to contact him as soon as possible, and using the telephone could have been even chancier than driving to his place of business. She didn't trust that the home telephone would not be tapped, and cell phone calls could be traced.

Cato had got up at his normal time and quietly dressed for work. She'd pretended to be asleep until he left the bedroom. Then, as soon as his car had cleared the driveway, she had dressed quickly and left the house, hoping to complete the errand and return home before Mrs. Berry arrived for the day.

Keeping a watchful eye in the rearview mirror, she'd been confident that no one had followed her. Despite her haste, she had heeded the speed limits, not wanting to be stopped for a traffic ticket that she would have to explain to Cato.

She had returned home only minutes ahead of the housekeeper and had remained in her bedroom ever since, pacing, playing over in her mind the events of the previous night, trying to decide what her next course of action should be.

Detective Bowen and Duncan Hatcher were waiting for her downstairs. She dreaded the interview, but further delay would look suspicious. She went to her dressing table, gathered her hair into a ponytail, considered changing clothes, then decided not to take the time. She picked up a tube of lip gloss, but changed her mind about that, too. Detective Bowen would find fault with her vanity, and Duncan Hatcher . . .

What did he think of her? she wondered. *Really* think of her.

She deliberated that for several precious moments, then, before she could talk herself out of it, did one thing more before leaving the bedroom.

The sunroom was a glass-enclosed portion of the terrace, floored in Pennsylvania bluestone, furnished with wicker pieces that had floral print cushions. Mrs. Berry was better with plants than with people. Ferns and palms and other potted tropicals flourished under her care.

When Elise entered the room, DeeDee Bowen was seated in one of the chairs facing the door. Duncan was standing at the wall of windows looking out over the terrace and swimming pool, seemingly captivated by the fountain at the center of it.

Detective Bowen stood up. "Hello, Mrs. Laird. We apologize for showing up unannounced. Is this an inconvenient time?"

"Not at all."

Upon hearing her name, Duncan turned away from the window. Elise glanced at him, then came into the room and joined Detective Bowen in the sitting area.

"Mrs. Berry will be here shortly with something to drink," she said, motioning Detective Bowen back into her chair, then sat down in one facing it.

"That'll be nice. It's so hot out."

"Yes."

Having exhausted the topic of the weather, they lapsed into an awkward silence. Elise was aware of Duncan, still standing near the window, watching her. She resisted looking in his direction.

Finally Bowen said, "We have a few more questions."

"Before leaving last night you implied that you would."

"Just a few things we'd like to clear up."

"I understand."

"Overnight, did you think of anything you left out? Something that may have slipped your mind?"

"No."

"That can happen in stressful situations." The woman smiled at her. "I've had people call me in the middle of the night, suddenly remembering a detail they'd forgotten."

"I told you what I remembered exactly as I remembered it."

The soft rattle of glassware announced the arrival of a serving cart, pushed into the room by Mrs. Berry. "Shall I serve, Mrs. Laird?" Her voice was as chilly as the condensation on the ice bucket. Elise wasn't sure if she was disdainful of their guests, or her. Probably both.

"No, thank you." Welcoming a chance to move and get out from under the scrutiny of the detectives, she left her chair and approached the cart. "I believe you prefer Diet Coke, Detective Bowen?"

"Sounds great."

Elise poured the cola over a glass of ice and carried it to her. She accepted it with an easy smile, which Elise instantly mistrusted. Then she turned and looked up at Duncan Hatcher. His eyes were still on her. Unblinking. Intent. "Something for you?"

He glanced at the cart. "Is that tea?"

"It's sweetened. Mrs. Berry thinks that's the only way to make it."

"That's the only way my mom makes it, too. Sweetened is fine." His smile was as easy as DeeDee Bowen's, but Elise trusted it even less. It never reached his eyes.

She wondered if the decision she'd made before coming downstairs was a foolhardy one.

Of course, it would have been more foolhardy not to do anything.

She poured Duncan Hatcher a glass of iced tea and was passing it to him when Cato strode into the room. "Apparently I didn't receive the memo."

CHAPTER
6

"Or did you just happen to be in the neighborhood?" the judge added with less civility.

Yep, he's angry, DeeDee thought. Just as Duncan had predicted he would be once he learned that they'd questioned his wife—or tried to—without his being present. They had the right to, of course, but had agreed to avoid ruffling the judge's feathers if at all possible.

Mrs. What's-her-name, the housekeeper, must have called him immediately upon their arrival, probably even before she went upstairs to tell Elise Laird they were here. It was clear that the domestic's loyalty lay with the judge and that she seemed to have little regard for his missus.

Elise offered to pour her husband a glass of tea.

"No, thank you." He kissed her on the lips, then pulled back and stroked her cheek. "How are you holding up?"

"Fine."

"Still shaken?"

"I think I will be for a while."

"Understandable."

He guided her down onto the settee that was barely wide enough to accommodate both of them, pulled her hand onto his knee, and covered it with his. "What would you like to know?"

DeeDee saw Duncan's jaw tense. He said, "I'd like to know if you want to call a lawyer before we begin. We'll be happy to wait until one arrives."

The judge replied crisply, "That won't be necessary. But to show up here unannounced was a cheap trick and, frankly, beneath you, Detective Hatcher."

"My apologies to you and to Mrs. Laird." Duncan sat down in one of the wicker armchairs facing the couple. "The name of the man who died in your study last night was Gary Ray Trotter."

Like Duncan, DeeDee closely watched their faces for any giveaway sign of recognition. There wasn't so much as a flicker, not in the judge's implacable stare, not in Elise Laird's limpid green eyes.

The judge glanced down at his wife. Reading his silent question, she shook her head. Looking back at them, he said, "We don't know him. I thought we'd made that clear to you last night."

"We hoped the name might jog your memory, remind you—"

"Obviously not, Detective Bowen," the judge said, cutting her off.

"A lot of people have been shuttled through your courtroom," Duncan said. "Trotter was a repeat offender. Perhaps he'd come before your bench."

"I would remember."

"You remember every party to every case you've ever tried?" DeeDee said. "Wow. That's impressive."

He fired another impatient glance at her, then addressed himself to Duncan. "He was a repeat offender? Then what more is there to discuss? This Trotter broke into my house, fired a handgun at my wife, forcing her to protect herself. Thank God her aim was better than his. He died, she didn't. Don't expect me to cry over him."

"I don't expect that at all."

The judge took a slow, deep breath as though to calm himself. "Then I guess I don't understand why you're here today. Why do you feel it necessary to make Elise relive this terrifying event?"

"We have some points that need clarification before we close the case," DeeDee said.

"Elise told you everything she had to tell you last night. As a judge who's heard years of courtroom testimony, I can honestly say that her account of what happened was comprehensive."

"I agree, and we appreciate her cooperation last night," DeeDee said to the couple, smiling at both. "Identifying Gary Ray Trotter has answered some of our outstanding questions, but created others, I'm afraid."

"Such as?"

DeeDee laughed softly. "Well, Judge, he wasn't a very accomplished crook. In fact, he was pretty much a loser, who couldn't even hack it as a criminal."

"So?"

"So Detective Hatcher and I were wondering why he chose your house to burglarize."

"I have no idea."

"Neither do we," DeeDee said bluntly. "Trotter had a criminal history dating back to adolescence. Robbery mostly. But he was a goof. For instance, he once walked into a convenience store with a stick in his pocket in lieu of a pistol and demanded the money in the till. But he paid for the gas he pumped into his getaway car with his sister's credit card."

The judge smiled wryly. "Which I think explains why he failed as a crook."

"I guess," DeeDee exclaimed on a short laugh. "I mean, last night he didn't even bring along gloves or robber paraphernalia of any kind. Can you believe that? Sort of makes you wonder, doesn't it?"

"What?"

Then she dropped her smile. "What the heck Gary Ray Trotter was doing in your study."

After a moment of taut silence, the judge said, "I know one thing he did. He tried to kill my wife."

Duncan pounced on that. "Which is another thing we must clear up, Mrs. Laird."

"What needs clearing up?" the judge asked.

"Are you absolutely certain that Trotter fired first?"

"Of course she's certain."

"I asked *her,* Judge."

"My wife has been through a terrible ordeal."

"And I've got a job to do," Duncan fired back. "That involves asking her some tough questions. If you haven't got the stomach for it, Judge, you can leave."

Elise held up her hand, stopping the judge from saying whatever he was about to say in response to Duncan's angry put-down. "Please, Cato. I want to answer their questions. I don't want there to be any doubt as to what happened." She had addressed her husband by name, but DeeDee noticed that her green gaze didn't waver from Duncan's face, nor his from hers.

"As I told you last night," she said, "when I accidentally switched on the foyer light—"

"Excuse me. Do you mind talking us through it where it happened?"

"In the study?"

"If it wouldn't be too much of an imposition."

"It will be very difficult for Elise to go into that room until it's been cleaned, rid of all reminders of what happened in it," the judge said.

"I realize it won't be easy," Duncan said. But he didn't withdraw the request.

The judge looked at his wife. "Elise?"

"I want to help in any way I can."

The four of them made their way into the foyer. Duncan approached the fancy console table. Beneath the marble top was a slender drawer that ran the width of the table. "You took the pistol from this drawer?"

"Yes, I came out of the butler's pantry through that door," she replied, pointing. "I paused there a moment. I didn't hear anything, but, as I told you last night, I sensed a presence in the study. I went to the table to get the pistol."

Duncan fingered one of the drawer pulls. "Did you make any noise?"

"I don't think so. I tried not to."

"Did you close the drawer?"

"I . . . I don't remember," she said, faltering. "I don't believe I did."

"She didn't," the judge said. "It was open when the first two policemen arrived in response to the 911. I remember pointing it out to them."

DeeDee made a mental note to read the report filed by Officers Beale and Crofton.

Duncan resumed. "You walked from the table to the door of the study."

"Yes."

"Were you wearing slippers?"

"I was barefoot."

"Do you think Trotter heard you approaching?" Duncan asked. "Or did he have no inkling you were there and aware of him until the light came on?"

"If he'd heard me coming toward the study, why didn't he just scramble out the window?"

"That was going to be my next question," Duncan said with a guileless smile.

"Then I must have startled him by switching on the light," Elise said. "When it came on, he froze."

"This is the switch plate?" Duncan flipped one switch, and the overhead light in the study came on. The other turned on a fixture in the foyer directly above their heads. He looked up at the light, then into the study. "DeeDee, would you play Trotter? Go stand behind the desk."

She peeled away the crime scene tape that formed an X in the open doorway, then went into the study and took a position behind the desk.

Duncan said, "Is that about where he was standing?"

Elise replied with a slight nod.

"What was he doing, Mrs. Laird?"

"Nothing. Only standing there looking at me. Staring, like a deer caught in headlights."

"Was he leaning over the desk, like he'd been trying to jimmy the lock on the drawer?"

"It took several seconds for my eyes to adjust to the sudden brightness. Maybe he was bending over the desk drawer, I don't know. The first mental picture I have of him is his standing there behind the desk, looking at me, motionless."

"Huh." Duncan looked toward DeeDee behind the desk as though imagining Gary Ray Trotter. "And what was it he said?" He came back around to Elise.

She didn't flinch and she didn't hesitate. "He didn't say anything, Detective Hatcher. I told you that last night."

Duncan nodded slowly. "Right. You did. But you spoke to him, correct? You ordered him to leave."

"Yes."

"Did he make a move toward the window?"

"No. He didn't move at all except to raise his arm. Suddenly. Like a string attached to his elbow had been yanked."

"Like this?" DeeDee demonstrated the motion.

"Something like that, yes. And before it even registered with me that he was holding a pistol, he fired it." She placed a hand at her throat as though suddenly finding it difficult to breathe.

The judge moved closer and slid his arm around her waist.

Duncan asked, "Mrs. Laird, is it possible that he was firing a warning shot, meant only to try and scare you?"

"I suppose it's possible."

"Did you feel in mortal danger?"

"I assumed I was. It all happened very fast."

"But not so fast that you didn't have time to 'assume' that you were in mortal danger."

"That's a reasonable assumption, isn't it, Detective?" the judge asked, sounding vexed. "If a man who's broken into your house fires a pistol, even if his aim is lousy, isn't it logical to assume that your life is in danger and to act accordingly?"

"It seems logical, yes," DeeDee said. "But Dr. Brooks had another theory worth considering. He suggested that maybe Trotter was falling backward when he fired his pistol, that reflexively his finger clenched on the trigger. That would explain his aim being so far off."

Duncan was staring hard at Elise. "But that would mean that you had shot at him first."

"But she didn't," the judge said. "She's told you that a dozen times. Why do you keep hammering away at this?"

Duncan tore his gaze from Elise Laird's stricken face and looked at the judge. "Because I've got to have a clear understanding of what happened. I dislike having to put these questions to Mrs. Laird. But I was there this morning when the autopsy was performed on Gary Ray Trotter's corpse. I feel I owe it to him, crook or not, to determine how and why he wound up like that. You're a public official, Judge. You have an obligation to the public to do your duty. So do I. Sometimes it's no fun at all. In fact, most of the time it's not."

He turned back to Elise. "Are you absolutely certain that Trotter fired at you first?"

"Absolutely."

"There. That ends it." The judge's statement was followed by a tense stretch of silence. Finally he said, "I admire your sense of duty, Detective Hatcher. I appreciate your quest for the truth. Elise and I have done everything within our power to help you perform your unpleasant duties.

"Haven't you stopped to consider that we would like a full explanation for what happened here last night, too? We would like that perhaps even more than you and Detective Bowen. Elise has been as straightforward as she could possibly be. Are you now satisfied that it was a break-in that went awry?"

Duncan let the question hover there for at least fifteen seconds before answering, "I believe so, yes."

My ass, thought DeeDee.

The judge said, "Good. Then if that's all, I hope you'll excuse us." He turned, ready to escort them out, when Elise forestalled him.

"I'd like to know . . ." Her voice cracked. She swallowed, tried again. "I'd like to know if Trotter had a family. A wife, children?"

"No," Duncan said. "His closest relative was an uncle up in Maryland."

"I'm glad of that. I would have hated . . . that."

"May I show you out now?" The judge started down the hall, expecting them to follow.

DeeDee came from behind the desk. As she moved past Elise, Elise reached for her hand. "Detective Bowen, I want to echo what my husband said. I know you're only doing your job."

Surprised by the move, DeeDee tried to think of something neutral to say that would be a fitting response, whether Elise was lying or telling the truth. "This can't be easy for you, either."

"It isn't, but if I think of anything to add, I promise to call you."

"That would be helpful."

"Do you have a business card?"

"Right here." Duncan plucked one from the breast pocket of his jacket and passed it to her.

"Thank you, Detective Hatcher." Taking the card, she shook hands with him, too.

DeeDee was as bouncy as one of those fuzzy orange dogs that look like manic powder puffs. An ex-girlfriend had owned one. The damn thing had barked nonstop. Most hyper animal Duncan had ever been around. Until today. DeeDee was practically jumping out of her skin.

"She's hiding something, Duncan. I know it. I feel it in my bones."

DeeDee's "bones" were rarely wrong. In this particular case, he hoped they were. He wanted to close this case with dispatch and remain in the judge's good graces. He'd never been a big fan of Judge Cato Laird, believing that often he talked out both sides of his mouth. Tough on crime and criminals one day, favoring the protection of their civil rights the next. His opinions seemed to drift along with the ebb and flow of public opinion, adhering only to the majority rule of the moment.

Duncan couldn't admire a man to whom popularity was more important than conviction, but he supposed in order to win elections, the judge had to practice politics. And he certainly didn't want a superior court judge as an enemy. That's what he was likely to become if he continued hassling the judge's wife because of what his partner felt in her bones.

Unfortunately, his bones were feeling the same thing. Especially after that last interview.

He jerked the steering wheel to the right and crossed two lanes of traffic to the accompaniment of blaring horns and shouted invectives. DeeDee gripped the armrest of the passenger door.

"What are you doing?"

"I'm thirsty." The car jounced over the curb as he came close to missing the entrance to a McDonald's.

"You had sweetened iced tea. 'Mrs. Berry thinks that's the only way to make it,' " she said, batting her eyelashes and mocking Elise Laird's drawl.

"I was *served* iced tea. I didn't drink it. Besides, aren't you overdue a shot of caffeine? Not that you need it," he added under his breath as he leaned toward the speaker to place their order.

"Should we go back and talk to some of the neighbors?" DeeDee asked.

"What good would that do? They were canvassed last night. None reported a recent burglary or break-in. No one saw Gary Ray Trotter lurking around the neighborhood. Nobody heard anything out of the ordinary last night."

"Maybe Mrs. Laird opened the door and invited him in."

"That's a real stretch, DeeDee."

After picking up their drinks at the window, he got back onto the street and rapidly closed in on the bumper of a soccer mom's van. "What is with everybody today?" he said as he went around the van. "People are driving like there's ice on the road."

"What's your hurry?" DeeDee asked.

He whipped into another lane in order to go around a slow-moving parochial school bus. "No hurry. I just hate this damn traffic."

Heedless of his complaining, DeeDee said, "Okay, so maybe she didn't welcome Trotter like a guest; there's still something wrong with that picture."

"I'll bite. What makes you think so?"

"Generally—"

"Don't be general. Be specific."

"Okay. Specifically, her reaction when you raised the question of her firing her pistol ahead of Trotter. She went whey-faced."

He supposed that "whey-faced" was one way to accurately describe Elise's expression. "I pushed pretty hard. She stuck to her story."

"Most good liars do."

"You think she's lying?"

"Maybe not lying," DeeDee said. "Just not telling the truth, the whole truth, and nothing but the truth."

"You're getting general again. Give me an example."

"I don't know. I can't be specific," she said, matching his irritability. "She just doesn't act like a woman who killed a hapless burglar last night."

"She didn't know he was hapless. Gary Ray Trotter didn't look like a screwup when he was standing in her house, in the dark, firing a weapon at her. Do you think she should have waited to shoot him until after she'd seen his résumé?"

His sarcasm earned him a glare.

"And she was concerned enough to ask if Trotter had a family," he pointed out. "It bothered her to think she might have orphaned some kids."

"I'll admit that was a nice touch."

"Why do you think it was a 'touch'?"

"Why are you defending her?"

"I'm not."

"Sure sounds like it to me."

"Well, it sounds to me like you're doing just the opposite. You think everything she says and does is disingenuous."

"Not everything. For instance, I believe that she was barefoot."

This time, she was on the receiving end of a baleful look.

"All I'm saying," she continued, "is that I believe the sweet remark about Trotter's family was made for your benefit."

"*My* benefit?"

"Oh, please, Duncan. Wake up. She answers my questions, but whenever she wants to stress a point, such as her truthfulness, she looks at you."

"You're imagining that."

"Like hell, I am. The lady knows on which side to butter her bread."

"Meaning?"

"You're a man."

"Which, in the context of this discussion, is beside the point."

"Right." She used the tone she did whenever he denied knowing how to play the piano. For the next several moments, she was deep in thought, poking at the ice cubes in her drink with her straw. "You know what else? I think suspicion has reared its ugly head to the judge."

"Now I know you're seeing things that aren't there," he said. "He's never more than half a foot away from her, treats her like she's made of porcelain."

"True. He's very protective. Almost as though he's afraid she might need his protection."

"He's her husband."

"He's also a judge who's listened to hours of sworn testimony in his courtroom, as he reminded us today. He commended her comprehensive recall. But you can bet he also knows a lie when he hears one. And he got awfully defensive when we advanced Dothan's theory about Trotter having been shot and reflexively pulling the trigger on his way down. Judge Laird pooh-poohed it without further explanation or discussion. His wife didn't fire first. Period. The end." She paused for breath. "Which leads me to believe that His Honor may be questioning his wife's story."

They arrived at the Barracks. Duncan pulled his car into a slot in the parking lot, but neither of them made a move to get out. He leaned forward, crossed his arms over the steering wheel, and stared through the windshield at the civilians and police personnel going in and out of the Habersham Street entrance.

He felt DeeDee's eyes on him, but he let her be the first to break the weighty silence. "Look, Duncan, I know it's hard to get past that face. That body. Although I know there's been speculation about my sexual orientation from yahoos like Worley, I'm straight. But being straight doesn't make me blind to Elise Laird's appeal. I can appreciate—okay, appreciate and *envy*—the way she looks and the effect she has on the opposite sex. There, I've been honest. Now you, in turn, must be honest with me."

She paused, but when he said nothing, she continued. "Can you honestly, cross-your-heart-and-hope-to-die honestly, be objective when you look at her?"

"I'm a cop."

"With a penis. And that particular organ is notorious for having lapses in judgment."

He turned and looked at her then. "Have you ever, *ever* known me to compromise an investigation?"

"No. With you it's either wrong or right, black or white, no gray areas. That's why as soon as I made detective I petitioned hard to become your partner."

"So where's this coming from?"

"We've never investigated a case involving a woman that you're attracted to. And you were attracted to Elise Laird the instant you saw her at the awards dinner. You can't deny that."

"She was a pretty face in the crowd."

"Who you compared to a lightning strike."

"That was before I knew her name. It was for sure as hell before she shot and killed a man."

"So your attraction to her died along with Trotter? No lingering groin tugs in that direction?"

He used his thumb to whisk beads of sweat off his forehead. "The lady is poison, DeeDee. Don't you think I know that?"

Her frown told him that wasn't exactly a direct answer to her question and that she still needed convincing.

"First of all," he said, "she's married."

"To a man you despise."

"Irrelevant."

"I wonder."

"Irrelevant," he repeated with emphasis. DeeDee didn't come back with further argument, but she still looked doubtful. He said, "I've had my share of girlfriends and short-term bed partners."

"An understatement."

"Name one who was married."

She stayed silent.

"Exactly," he said. "I've massaged the issue of sexual morality to fit my lifestyle and to satisfy the urge of the moment, but I draw the line at adultery, DeeDee."

She nodded. "Okay, I believe you. But if she wasn't married—"

"She's still a principal in an active investigation."

DeeDee's face brightened. "*Active*. Does that mean we're not closing the book on it just yet?"

"No," he said heavily. "Not yet. Like you, I sense there's some-thing out of joint."

"It's her. She's . . . what was your fifty-cent word? Disin-genuous?"

"The background check you ran on her didn't produce much, did it?"

She ticked off on her fingers the facts she'd learned about Elise Laird. "She has no arrest record, no outstanding debts, and there was nothing printed about her in the local newspaper before she married Laird. She came out of nowhere."

"Nobody comes out of nowhere."

DeeDee thought about it for a moment. "I've got a friend with ties to the society set. Often the best source of information is good old-fashioned gossip."

"Keep the inquiry discreet."

"I won't even have to ask for info. Once I mention Elise Laird's name, I bet I get an earful. This friend thrives on gossip."

They got out, but as they approached the steps of the entrance, Duncan continued down the sidewalk. DeeDee asked where he was going.

"I'm days overdue calling my folks. I can talk to them easier out here than in the office with all the commotion."

She went inside. Duncan followed the sidewalk around to the front of the building that faced Oglethorpe Avenue, walked past the black-and-white 1953 squad car that was parked out front like a mascot, and continued on until he reached the middle of the block, where there was a gated entrance to the Colonial Park Cemetery.

A few stalwart tourists braving the afternoon heat were taking pictures, reading the historical plaques, and trying to decipher the in-scriptions carved into the grave markers. He made his way to one of the shaded wood benches and sat down, but he didn't reach for his cell phone to call his parents. Instead he sat there and stared at the leaning headstones and crumbling brick vaults.

He could imagine the ghosts of fallen Revolutionary War heroes staring back at him expectantly, waiting to see what he would do. Would he do what he knew to be right? Or, for the first time in his ca-reer, would he violate the dictates of his conscience?

Above the nearby rooftops were the twin spires of St. John the Baptist cathedral, serving as another reminder that to transgress was a matter of choice.

Despite these silent warnings, he reached into his trousers pocket and withdrew the note he'd put there after having it surreptitiously slipped to him by Elise Laird when they shook hands.

He'd felt it immediately, sandwiched between their palms. She'd clasped his hand tightly so the note couldn't fall to the floor and give her away. Her eyes had begged him not to.

Despite her pleading gaze, he should have acknowledged the note right then. If not immediately, then surely as soon as he and DeeDee were alone. He should have told his partner about it, opened it, read it for the first time along with her.

But he hadn't.

Now, it seemed as hot as a cinder lying in his palm. He turned it over several times, examining it. The single white sheet had been folded over twice to form a small square. It weighed practically nothing. It looked innocuous enough, but he knew better. No matter what it said, it meant trouble for him.

If it contained information on last night's shooting, it amounted to evidence, which he was already guilty of withholding.

If it was personal, well, that would be even more compromising.

The first instance would be a legal matter. The second, a moral one.

It wasn't too late to show it to DeeDee now. He could invent an excuse for not having shown it to her sooner, which she probably wouldn't believe but would readily accept because she would be so curious to read the contents of the note. They would open it, read it, and together analyze its meaning.

Short of that, and almost as honorable an action, he could destroy it and go to his grave wondering what it had said.

Instead, with damp hands, shortness of breath, and a rapidly beating heart, with the spirits of the nation's founders watching with stern disapproval, and the church spires pointing heavenward as though bringing his error to God's attention, he slowly unfolded the note. The words had been written in a neat script.

I must see you alone. Please.

CHAPTER
7

ELISE WAS WATCHING A MOVIE ON DVD. IT WAS THE FILM version of a Jane Austen novel. She'd seen it at least a dozen times and could practically quote the dialogue. The costumes and sets were lavish. The cinematography was gorgeous. The tribulations suffered by the heroine were superficial and easily solved. The outcome was happy.

Unlike real life. Which is why she liked the story so well.

"I was right," Cato announced as he entered the den, where there was a wide-screen TV and her sizable library of DVDs.

She reached for the remote and muted the audio. "About what?"

He sat down beside her on the sofa. "Gary Ray Trotter was never in my courtroom. As soon as the detectives left, I called my office and ordered that the records be searched. Thoroughly. I never presided over the trial of a Gary Ray Trotter."

"Would you know if he was ever called as a witness in another trial?"

"Determining that would take more man-hours than I'm willing to invest. Besides, I'm almost certain that what I told the detectives is correct. I'd never seen the man before. You said you didn't recognize him either."

"I said it because it's true."

After a beat, he said, "I didn't mean to imply otherwise, Elise."

"I'm sorry. I didn't mean to sound so short."

"You have reason to be." He kissed her gently. When they pulled apart, she asked if he would like a drink. "I'd love one, thank you."

She went to the small wet bar, picked up a heavy crystal decanter of scotch, and tilted the spout against a highball glass.

"Do you know Robert Savich?"

Elise nearly dropped the decanter. "I'm sorry, what?"

"Savich. Ever hear of him?"

She redirected her attention to pouring scotch. "Hmm, the name sounds vaguely familiar."

"It should. He's in the news now and again. He's a drug kingpin. Among other things."

Keeping her expression impassive, she plunked two cubes of ice into his drink, carried it with her back to the sofa, and passed it to him. "I hope it's to your liking."

He took a sip, pronounced it perfect, and kept his eyes trained on her over the top of the glass. "Savich is the reason Hatcher is being so rough on you."

She picked up a throw pillow and hugged it against her chest. "What does one have to do with the other?"

"Remember I told you that I'd found Hatcher in contempt of court and put him in jail?"

"You said he was upset over a mistrial."

"Savich's."

"Oh."

"Detective Hatcher is still holding a grudge against me," Cato said. "You're catching the brunt of it."

She threaded the fringe on the pillow through her fingers. "He's only doing his job."

"I grant that he has to ask difficult questions in any investigation, but he's had you on the defensive from the get-go. His partner, too."

"Detective Bowen doesn't like me at all."

"Jealousy," he said with a dismissive gesture. "She's pea green with it, and one can clearly see why. But she's insignificant."

"That's not the impression I get," Elise murmured, remembering the suspicion with which the other woman had looked at her, last night and today.

"Bowen has earned some commendations, as you know. But Hatcher is the standard by which she measures herself." Chuckling, he rattled the ice cubes in his glass. "And he's a tough yardstick."

"What do you mean?"

"He's smart, and he's an honest cop. Bowen looks up to him. His allies are hers. That goes double for his enemies."

"I doubt he thinks of you as an enemy, Cato."

"Maybe that word is a bit strong, but he has a long-standing gripe with me, and now he's taking it out on you."

"There's more water under the bridge than this recent mistrial?"

"I've heard of his rumblings. He thinks I'm not tough enough." He shrugged as if the criticism didn't concern him. "That's a common complaint from hard-nosed cops."

"He's hardly Dirty Harry."

He smiled at her analogy. "No, he's not *that* hard-nosed. In fact, the man's a contradiction. Once, when he was testifying at the trial of an accused child killer, he got tears in his eyes when he described the crime scene, the small body of the victim. To see him that day on the witness stand, you'd think he was a softie.

"But I've heard that he assumes another personality when he's questioning a suspect, particularly when he knows the suspect is lying or giving him the runaround. It's said he can lose his temper and even get physical." He stroked her hair. "You got a glimpse of that side of him today, didn't you?"

"I never felt physically threatened," she said, only half in jest.

Cato responded in kind. "He wouldn't dare. But the way he was questioning you about who fired first, you or that Trotter character, bordered on harassment." He sipped his drink thoughtfully. "A call to his supervisor, Bill Gerard, or even to Chief Taylor may be in order."

"Please don't."

Her sharp tone surprised him. "Why not?"

"Because . . ." She stopped to think of a plausible answer. "Because I don't want to draw attention to the incident. I don't want more made of it than already has been."

Studying her, he set his drink on the coffee table and curved his hand around her neck. His fingers were very cold. "What are you afraid of, Elise?"

Her heart somersaulted, but she managed to form a puzzled smile. "I'm not afraid."

"Are you afraid that the questions Hatcher and Bowen are asking about last night may lead to . . . something? Something uglier than what happened?"

"What could be uglier than a man *dying?*"

He studied her for several seconds, then smiled at her tenderly. "You're right. Never mind. Silly thought." He released her and stood up. "Finish your movie. Would you like Mrs. Berry to bring you something?"

She declined with a shake of her head.

He picked up his highball glass and carried it with him. At the door, he turned back. "Darling?"

"Yes?"

"If you hadn't been downstairs last night, this incident would have been avoided. Trotter may have burglarized us, but that wouldn't have been the end of the world. Everything is well insured. Perhaps from now on, you should confine your strolls through the house in the middle of the night to the upper floor."

She gave him a weak smile. "That's probably a good idea."

He returned her smile and seemed about to go, when he hesitated a second time. "You know . . . another reason for Hatcher's badgering."

"What?"

"It gives him an excuse to look at you." He chuckled. "Poor bastard."

Duncan was in his office, seated at his littered desk, shuffling through telephone messages, trying to look busy for the benefit of DeeDee and the other detectives who were at their desks that afternoon, and wishing like hell that he'd never opened that note.

He couldn't guess at Elise Laird's purpose for passing it to him. But the result was that it had convinced him that her explanation for the shooting of Gary Ray Trotter was bogus. There was more to it than the luck of a dumb crook finally running out. If it had been strictly a matter of self-defense, she wouldn't be slipping a note to the detective overseeing the investigation, asking him to meet her alone.

Which was not going to happen.

It *wasn't*.

He pushed aside the unanswered telephone messages, propped his feet on top of his desk, and reached for a yellow legal tablet on which to jot down thoughts as they came to him.

In addition to the note, there were other reasons he—and DeeDee—found Elise Laird's story hard to accept. One was the burglary itself. It seemed odd that Trotter was on foot in a classy neighborhood like Ardsley Park. The residential area was demarcated by busy boulevards, but the streets within the area didn't invite pedestrians other than moms pushing baby strollers or people out getting their exercise. A man walking the streets a half hour after midnight would arouse immediate suspicion. A seasoned crook—even an unsuccessful one—would know that and have a getaway car parked nearby.

Also, it was an outlandish coincidence that Trotter had chosen to break into that house on the one night, out of all nights, that Mrs. Laird had forgotten to engage the alarm system.

Okay, so wine and sex could make you lazy. But her satiation hadn't overcome her insomnia. She hadn't drifted off into a peaceful, postcoital slumber. No, she'd gone downstairs for a glass of milk to help her fall asleep. Wouldn't roaming around in the dark house have reminded her that she had failed to set the alarm?

Second, when she heard a noise coming from the study, why hadn't she crept back into the kitchen and used the telephone to dial 911? Why had her first reaction been to grab a pistol and confront the intruder?

Third, Trotter didn't seem like a guy who would brazen it out if caught red-handed. He seemed the type to tuck tail and get the hell outta there. Only a supremely confident burglar would stick around and have a face-off, especially if he was there only to steal something.

Duncan's mind stumbled over that thought. Mentally he backtracked and looked at it again. He underlined *if he was there only to steal something,* then drew a large question mark beside it.

"Hey, Dunk."

Another detective popped his head inside the door. His name was Harvey Reynolds, but everyone called him Kong because of his gorilla-like pelt. Every inch of exposed skin was covered in thick, curly black hair. No one dared speculate on what the unexposed parts of his body looked like.

His apelike appearance was further enhanced by his thick neck, barrel chest, and short legs. Despite his intimidating appearance, he couldn't be a nicer guy. He coached Little League for his twin sons' team and was dotty over his homely wife, believing himself lucky to have won such a prize as she. Duncan, who'd met the lady on several occasions, agreed with Kong. She was a prize. It was clear the couple were nuts about each other.

"Can I bend your ear for a minute?"

Duncan was eager to get back to examining that last niggling thought he'd written down, but he tossed the legal tablet onto his desk and motioned Kong in. "What's the Little League team selling this week? Candy bars? Magazine subscriptions?"

Kong gave him a good-natured grin. "Citrus fruit from the valley."

"What valley?"

"Beats the hell out of me. I'll hit you up for that later. This is business." Kong worked missing persons in the special victims unit, or SVU. Sometimes their cases overlapped. He pulled up a chair and straddled it backward, folding his hirsute arms over it. "Anything cooking on Savich since the mistrial?"

"Not even a simmer."

"Bitch of a turn."

"Tell me."

"He never got nailed for those other two ... uh ... Bonnet, wasn't it?"

"Yeah, and a guy named Chet Rollins before him," Duncan said tightly.

"Right. Wasn't ever indicted for those, was he?"

Duncan shook his head.

"I thought you had him for sure this time. Is he gonna get away with doing Freddy Morris, too?"

"Not if I can help it."

"Limp-dick DA," Kong muttered.

Duncan shrugged. "He says he's hamstrung till we come up with something solid."

"Yeah, but still . . . Feds have anything?"

"Not that I've heard."

"They still steamed?"

"Oh, yeah. Breaks my heart. They never call, never write."

Kong chuckled. "Well, anything that I can do to help you nail that son of a bitch Savich . . ."

"Thanks." Duncan hitched his chin at the sheet of paper in Kong's shaggy clutch. "What's up?"

"Meyer Napoli."

Duncan guffawed. "You must have been out overturning rocks today."

Meyer Napoli was well known to the police department. He was a private investigator who specialized in fleecing his clients of huge sums of money by doing practically nothing except making guarantees that he rarely fulfilled.

It wasn't unlike him to work both ends against the middle. If hired by a wife to get the goods on an unfaithful husband, Napoli was known to go to said husband and, for a fee, promise to return to the wife empty-handed. He also usually consoled the brokenhearted wife in a way that made her feel like a desirable woman again.

"Which rock did you find Napoli under?"

Kong tugged on his earlobe, from which a crop of black bristles sprouted. "Well, that's the problem. I didn't."

"Huh?"

"Napoli's secretary called us this morning, said Napoli failed to show up at his office for a meeting with a client. She called his house and his cell phone a dozen times apiece, but failed to raise him. That never happens. He stays in touch, she said. Always. No exceptions.

"So she went over to his place to see if he was dead or something. No trace of him. That's when she called us. She's been calling every hour since, insisting that something has happened to him. Said he wouldn't miss a morning of appointments with clients, no matter what. According to her, he never takes a sick day or vacation, and even if he did, he wouldn't without letting her know.

"She was bugging us so bad, hell, I gave in. I went over to his office and explained that unless there's evidence of foul play, we don't consider an adult officially missing unless it's been twenty-four hours since he was last seen. She said there was nothing at his house to indicate foul play, but something bad must've happened to him or else he'd be at work."

Duncan figured Kong had a good reason for telling him all this, and he wished he'd get to the point. His stomach had reminded him that it was past suppertime. It had been a very long day after a very short night. He was ready to take home some carry-out chicken, crack a beer, maybe play the piano to help him do some free associating about Trotter, specifically what he was doing in the Lairds' house and why he hadn't made a dash for it when he was caught.

He also needed to think about Elise Laird's note, why she'd given it to him, and why he hadn't shared it with his partner.

Kong was still talking. "I figured Napoli's private office would be sacrosanct. Locked down, you know? But his secretary was so flustered, she didn't notice that I was scanning the paperwork on his desk while she was wringing her hands, wondering where her boss is at."

At this point, Kong produced the sheet of paper he'd brought in with him. Duncan saw on it a typewritten list of names. "I memorized some of the names I saw on paperwork scattered across Napoli's desk," Kong explained. "Typed up this list soon as I got back to the office so I wouldn't forget them.

"Frankly, I figure Napoli dived underground to avoid somebody he's pissed off, either an irate, dissatisfied client or some broad he was banging. But if the scumbag *has* met with foul play—the secretary's convinced—I figured these names might come in handy. Gives us places to start looking for him."

Duncan nodded, indicating that he followed Kong's reasoning.

"Now, why I bring this up to you . . ." Kong pointed to a name about midway down the list. "Isn't this your guy?"

Duncan read the name. Moving slowly, he lowered his feet from his desk, took the sheet from Kong, and read it again. Then in a dry, scratchy voice, he said, "Yeah, that's my guy."

"It was scandalous. From meeting to altar took less than three months."

It was a short drive from the Barracks to Meyer Napoli's downtown office. DeeDee took advantage of it to share what she'd pieced together about Elise Laird's background.

"Short courtships aren't that unusual or scandalous," Duncan observed.

"Unless a distinguished superior court judge is marrying a cocktail waitress. Riiiiight," she drawled in response to Duncan's sharp look. "Elise worked the bar at Judge Laird's country club."

"Which is?"

"Silver Tide, naturally. Anyway, after meeting her, the judge began playing golf every single day, sometimes two rounds, but spent most of his time at the nineteenth hole."

Duncan parked at the curb in front of the squat, square office building and put a sign in his windshield identifying him as a cop to avoid getting a ticket from one of Savannah's infamous meter maids. He opened his car door and got out, hoping to catch a breeze. The air was motionless, suffocating. The sun had set, but heat still radiated up from the sidewalk, baking the soles of his shoes.

"Want to hear the skinny now or later?" DeeDee asked as they approached the door of the office building.

"Now."

"The judge was a confirmed bachelor who enjoyed casual affairs with widows and divorcées with no intention of getting married. Why share the family wealth? But Elise dazzled him. He fell hard. The gossip is she screwed him silly, got him addicted to her, then refused to sleep with him again unless and until he married her."

"What the hell's taking this elevator so long?" While the airconditioning inside the building was welcome, it did little to improve Duncan's crankiness, which he blamed on the sultry heat. He punched the up button on the elevator several times, but heard no grinding of gears indicating movement in the shaft. "Let's take the stairs. It's only two flights."

DeeDee followed him up the aggregate steps. Depressions had been worn into them by decades of foot traffic. This wasn't prize real estate. A smell of mildew clung to the old walls.

"The judge's friends and associates were shocked by the engagement," DeeDee said. "The rock he bought her—have you noticed it?"

"No."

"A marquise, reputedly six carats. I'd say that's a conservative estimate."

"You noticed?" Jewelry wasn't something DeeDee ordinarily paid attention to.

"I couldn't help but notice," she said to his back as they rounded the second-floor landing. "Damn near blinded me this afternoon when we were in the sunroom. Didn't you notice the rainbow it cast on the wall?"

"Guess I missed that."

"You were too busy gazing into her eyes."

He stopped in midstep and looked over his shoulder.

"Well, you were," she said defensively.

"I was questioning her. What was I supposed to do, keep my eyes shut?"

"Never mind. Just . . ." She motioned him forward. He continued climbing the stairs and she picked up her story. "So, the besotted judge throws himself this big, elaborate wedding. Under the circumstances, some thought it the height of tacky and tasteless, and attributed his extravagance to his greedy and demanding bride."

Duncan had reached the third-floor landing. Ahead was a corridor lined on both sides with doors to various offices. Names were stenciled in black on frosted glass. A CPA firm, an attorney, a dentist advertising fillings for the low, low price of twenty-five dollars. All were closed for the night. But one door about midway down stood open, casting a wedge of light into the otherwise dim hallway. He could hear Kong talking to Napoli's secretary. Her voice rose and fell emotionally.

Before joining them, he wished to finish this conversation with DeeDee. He turned to face her, blocking her path. "What 'circumstances'?"

"Pardon?"

"You said circumstances made the wedding tacky and tasteless."

"The bride had no pedigree, no family of any sort. At least none turned up at the wedding. She had no formal education, no property, no trust fund, no stock portfolio, nothing to recommend her. She brought nothing to the relationship except . . . well, the obvious.

"And she wore white. A simple dress, not too froufrou, but definitely white, which some considered the worst breach of etiquette. She did, however, order personalized stationery. Good stock, ivory in color, with the return address in dove gray lettering. She sent handwritten thank-you notes on behalf of her and the judge to everyone who gave them a wedding gift. And she has a very nice script."

Yeah. Duncan had seen her script. Scowling, he said, "Are you making this shit up?"

"No, swear to God."

"Where'd you get your information?"

"The friend I mentioned. We go all the way back to Catholic school. My folks had to roll coins to pay for my tuition. Her family is very well-to-do, but we formed a bond because both of us hated the school.

"Anyway, I called her up, mentioned the shooting at the Lairds' house, which she already knew about, because it's caused such a buzz. Her mom is definitely in the know, plugged into the society grapevine. If you're into this kind of stuff, she's a reliable source."

Duncan ran his sleeve across his forehead. The cloth came away wet. "Is there more? What color was the punch at the reception?"

She frowned at him, but continued. "Mrs. Laird never fails to RSVP to an invitation whether she's accepting or declining. Evidently she picked up a few social graces when she became Mrs. Cato Laird, and she's shown surprising good taste in clothes, but she's still considered *trash*—and that word was emphasized in an undertone. She's tolerated because of the judge, but she's far from accepted. You can forget embraced."

Duncan said, "You know what this sounds like to me? It sounds like Savannah's social set found an easy target for their malice. Here you have a bunch of snooty, jealous gossips who would give up their pedigree for Elise Laird's looks. They'd sacrifice Great-grandma's pearls in exchange for a chest like hers."

"Funny you should mention that particular attribute." DeeDee took the final steps necessary to join him on the landing. "The judge's circle of acquaintances might have overlooked her other shortcomings, even the fact that she worked in the bar at their country club. After all, it's an elite club, its membership limited to only the 'best people.' But what they couldn't forgive is what she was before becoming a cocktail waitress."

"Which was what?"

"A *topless* cocktail waitress."

CHAPTER
8

THE CREPE MYRTLE TREE WAS DRIPPING MOISTURE AND SO WAS Duncan. Elbows locked, his arms were braced against the smooth tree trunk, his body at an almost forty-five-degree angle from it as he stretched out his left calf muscle.

His head was hanging between his arms. Sweat dripped off his face onto the lichen-covered brick sidewalk in front of his town house. The sidewalk was buckled from roots of live oaks that lined the street and formed a canopy above it. He was grateful for the shade.

Breaking with tradition, he'd gotten up early and had decided to go for a run, before the sun was fully up, before it pushed the temperature from the eighties at six thirty into the nineties by nine. Even so, each breath had been a labored gasp. The air was as dense as chowder.

Most people were sleeping in this Saturday morning. In the next block a woman was watering the ferns on her porch. Earlier, Duncan had seen a man walking his dog in Forsyth Park. Few cars were on the streets.

He switched feet to stretch his other calf. His stomach growled, reminding him that he'd forgone the carry-out fried chicken last night, opting to come straight home after leaving Meyer Napoli's office. While there, he'd lost his appetite and had skipped supper altogether.

He'd tried to get interested in a baseball game on TV. When that failed, he moved to the piano, but his playing had been uninspired and for once hadn't helped him sort through his disturbing thoughts. He'd slept in brief snatches between long periods of wakefulness. Still restless at dawn, he'd kicked off the annoying bedsheet and gotten up, his mind in as much of a tangle as it had been the previous evening.

"Detective Hatcher?"

With a start, he turned. She was standing no more than three feet away. His heart rate, which during his stretches had returned to a normal, post-exercise rhythm, spiked at the sight of her.

He looked past her, almost expecting someone to be there playing a practical joke on him. He couldn't have been more surprised had there been a rowdy group with balloons and noisemakers having fun at his expense.

But the sidewalk was empty. The woman who'd been watering her ferns was no longer on her porch. There was no sight of the dog and his owner. Nothing, not a single leaf, moved in the thick air. Only his rushing breath disturbed it.

"What the hell are you doing here?"

"Didn't you read my note?" she said.

"Yeah, I read it."

"Well then."

"It's a bad idea for us to meet alone. In fact, this meeting just concluded."

He moved toward the steps of his town house, but she sidestepped to block his path. "Please don't walk away. I'm desperate to talk to you."

"About the fatal shooting at your house?"

"Yes."

"All right. I'm interested to hear what you have to say. I have an office. Give me half an hour. Detective Bowen and I will meet you there."

"No. I need to speak to you privately. Just you."

He steeled himself against her soft-spoken urgency. "You can talk to me at the police station."

"No, I can't. This is too sensitive to talk about there."

Sensitive. A bothersome word for sure. He said, "The only thing you and I have to talk about is a dead and dissected Gary Ray Trotter."

A few strands of pale hair had shaken loose from a messy top-knot. The hairdo looked like an afterthought, something she had fashioned as she rushed out the door. She was dressed in a snug cotton T-shirt and a full skirt that hung from a wide band around her hips, the hem skimming her knees. Leather flip-flops on her feet. It was a typical summertime outfit, nothing special about it, except that she was the woman inside, giving shape to the ordinary clothing.

She nodded toward the steps leading up to his front door. "Can we go inside?"

"Not a chance."

"I can't be seen with you," she exclaimed.

"Damn right you can't. You should have thought of that before you came. How'd you get here anyway?"

"I parked my car on Jones."

One street over. That's how she'd managed to come up behind him unheard and unseen until she'd wanted to be. "How'd you know where I live?"

"Telephone directory. I thought the A. D. Hatcher listed might be you. What's the *A* for?" When he didn't respond, she said, "I took a huge risk by coming here."

"You must enjoy taking risks. Like passing me the note practically under your husband's nose."

"Yes, I risked Cato seeing it, and I risked you giving me away. But you didn't. Did you show my note to Detective Bowen?"

He felt his face grow warm and refused to answer.

"I didn't think you would," she said softly.

Embarrassed and angry, he said, "What did you do, sneak out on the judge this morning? Leave him sleeping in your bed?"

"He had an early tee time." She came a step closer. "You've got to help me. Please."

She didn't touch him, but she might as well have for the heat that gathered in his crotch. *"Groin tug,"* he remembered DeeDee saying. Pretty accurate description. He wished he was dressed in something more substantial than nylon running shorts.

"I will help you," he said evenly. "It's my duty as a law officer to help you, as well as to resolve the case involving you. But not here and not now. Give me time to clean up. I'll call Detective Bowen. We'll set a time to meet. Doesn't have to be at the police station. You name the place, we'll be there."

Before he was finished, she had lowered her head and was shaking it remorsefully. "You don't understand." She spoke barely loud enough for him to hear. "I can't talk about this to anyone else."

"Why me?"

She raised her head then and looked up at him meaningfully. Their gazes locked and held. Understanding passed between them. The air shimmered with more than thermal heat.

For Duncan, everything receded except her face. Those eyes, as bottomless as the swimming hole he used to dive into headfirst, although he'd been warned that doing so was reckless. That mouth. Shaped as though giving pleasure was its specialty.

Suddenly the front door of the neighboring town house opened, alarming them. Elise slipped into the recessed doorway beneath his front steps where she couldn't be seen.

"Good morning, Duncan," the neighbor lady called as she retrieved her newspaper from the porch. "You're up mighty early."

"Getting in my exercise before it gets too hot."

"My, my, you're disciplined. But, honey, you be careful of this heat. Don't overexert yourself, now."

"I won't."

She retreated into her house and closed the front door. He ducked below the steps into the damp, cavelike enclosure, surprisingly cool and dim. It served as the entrance to a basement apartment that he had rented out when he'd first acquired the town house. His last renter had skipped out, owing him three months' rent. He hadn't bothered to lease it again. He missed the additional income, but rather liked having all four floors of the town house to himself.

Elise stood in shadow with her back pressed against the door.

"I want you away from here," he whispered angrily. "Now. And don't pass me any more notes. What is this, junior high? I don't know what your game is—"

"Gary Ray Trotter came to our house to kill me."

Duncan's rapid breathing sounded loud in the semi-enclosed area. The top of his head barely cleared the low brick ceiling, where ferns sprouted from cracks in the mortar. There was scarcely room enough for two people in the confined space. He was standing close enough to feel the hem of her skirt against his legs, her breath on his bare chest.

"What?"

"I shot him in self-defense. I had no choice. If I hadn't, he would have killed me. That's what he was sent to do. He'd been hired to kill me." She'd spoken in a rush, causing the words to stumble over one another. When she finished, she paused and drew in a short but deep breath.

Duncan stared at her while he pieced together her hurried words so they would make sense. But even after making sense of them, he couldn't believe them. "You can't be serious."

"Do I look like I'm joking?"

"Trotter was a hired assassin?"

"Yes."

"Hired by who?"

"My husband."

His phone was ringing as he ushered—more like pushed—Elise through the front door. He went around her and snatched up the phone, looking directly at her as he raised it to his ear. "Yeah?"

"Are you up?" DeeDee asked.

"Yeah."

"You sound out of breath."

"Just got in from a run."

"I've had some ideas about what we learned last night."

He continued to stare at Elise with single-minded concentration. She was watching him with equal intensity.

"Duncan?"

"I'm still here." He hesitated, then said, "Look, DeeDee, I'm dripping sweat, about to melt all over the living room floor. Let me shower, then I'll call you back."

"Okay, but be quick."

As he disconnected, he realized that he'd made another ill-advised decision. Already he'd placed himself in a dangerously gray area by not telling DeeDee about the note. Now he'd omitted to tell her who was in his living room, making unreasonable claims about a crime they were investigating. In both instances, he had violated police procedure and his personal code of ethics. Somewhere along the way he knew he would be held accountable.

It made him terribly angry at the woman responsible for his misconduct and for the conflicting emotions that assailed him every time he was near her. And even when he wasn't.

As he dropped the phone back onto the end table, she said huskily, "Thank you."

"Don't thank me yet. I'm still a cop with a dead man in the morgue, and you're the lady with a smoking gun in her hand."

"Then why didn't you tell your partner that I'm here?"

"I'm feeling generous this morning," he said, with much more flippancy than he felt. "Especially toward damsels in distress." In a measured tread, he walked toward her. To her credit she stood her ground and didn't back away. "That's the angle you're playing, isn't it?"

"I'm not playing an angle. I came to you because I don't know what else to do."

"Because you see me as a sucker."

"You're a policeman!"

"Who said he wanted to fuck you!"

She was taken aback by his bluntness, but recovered quickly. "You told me that remark had more to do with my husband than with me."

"It did," he said, wondering if she believed that. Wondering if *he* did. He continued forward, forcing her to walk backward. "But when you got yourself in a jam, you remembered it. You killed a man, for reasons yet to be discovered. But, lucky you, the detective investigating the fatal shooting thinks you look good enough to eat."

By now he had her against the wall, and they were standing toe to toe. He planted his hand near her head and leaned in close. "So to turn me all squishy with sympathy and blind to your guilt, you invent this story about a killer for hire."

"It's not a story. It's the truth."

"Judge Laird wants an instant divorce?"

"No, he wants me to *die*."

The conviction with which she spoke gave Duncan momentary pause. She took advantage of it to step around him. "Maybe you should rinse off."

"Sorry. You'll just have to put up with the stink."

"You don't smell bad, but doesn't the drying sweat itch?"

Reflexively he scratched the center of his chest. The hair there had become matted and salty. "I can stand it."

"I'll be glad to wait for—"

"Why does your husband want you dead?" he asked, speaking over her. "And why is it a big secret you can only tell me?"

She closed her eyes briefly, then opened them and said, "I came to you with this, sought you out personally, because I sensed you would be more—"

"Gullible?"

"Receptive. Certainly more so than Detective Bowen."

"Because I'm a man and she's a woman?"

"Your partner comes across as hostile. For whatever reason, our chemistry isn't very good."

"By contrast, you think our chemistry is?"

She lowered her gaze. "I felt . . . I thought . . ." When she raised her head and looked at him, her eyes were imploring. "Will you at least listen with an open mind?"

He folded his arms over his chest, fully realizing that it was a subconscious, self-protective gesture. When she looked at him like that, her eyes seemed to touch him, and his physical reactions were as though she actually had.

"Okay, I'm listening. Why does your husband want you dead?"

She took a moment, as though collecting her thoughts. "You and Detective Bowen picked up on the alarm not being set."

"Because you and the judge had sex."

"Yes. After, I tried to get up and set the alarm. But Cato wouldn't let me leave the bed. He pulled me back down and . . ."

"I get the picture. He was horny."

She didn't like that remark. Her expression changed, but she didn't address his vulgarity. "Cato didn't want the alarm to be set that night. He wanted Trotter to get into the house. After I was dead, he could truthfully say that it was part of my routine to set the alarm and that he had prevented me from doing so. He would say that he would never forgive himself, that if only he had allowed me to leave the bed, the tragedy would have been prevented. He would assume responsibility for my murder and, by doing so, win everyone's pity. It's a brilliant strategy. Don't you see?"

"Yeah, I see. But when you were in the kitchen and heard the noise, why didn't you call 911, get help immediately?"

"I didn't know how much time I had." She answered quickly, as though she'd known he would ask that and needed to have a response ready. "My instinct was to protect myself. So I took the pistol from the drawer in the foyer table."

Duncan tugged on his lower lip as though thinking it through. "You wanted the pistol in case Trotter attacked before you could make the 911 call."

"I suppose that's what I was thinking. I'm not sure I was thinking at all. I merely reacted. I was afraid."

She dropped down onto the piano bench and covered her face with her hands, massaging her forehead with the pads of her fingers. This position left the nape of her neck exposed and Duncan's gaze found it, just as it had the night of the awards dinner. He blinked away the vision of kissing her there.

"You were afraid," he said, "but you found the courage to go into the study."

"I don't know where I got the courage. I think maybe I hoped I was wrong. I hoped that what I'd heard was a tree branch knocking against the eaves, or a raccoon on the roof, something. But I knew that wasn't it. I knew that someone was in there, waiting for me.

"I'd been expecting it for several months. Not a burglary, specifically. But *something*. This was the moment I'd been dreading." She pressed her fist against the center of her chest, right above her heart, pulling the fabric of her T-shirt tight across her breasts. "I knew, Detective. I knew." Whispering that, she raised her head and looked up at him. "Gary Ray Trotter wasn't a thief I caught in the act. He was there to kill me."

Duncan pinched the bridge of his nose and closed his eyes as though concentrating hard, trying to work out the details in his mind. Actually, he had to do something to keep from drowning in those damn eyes of hers or becoming fixated on her breasts. He wanted to haul her up against him, kiss her, and see if her mouth delivered as promised. Instead, he pinched the skin between his eye sockets until it hurt like hell. It helped him to refocus. Some.

"Gary Ray Trotter hardly fits the profile of a hired assassin. Mrs. Laird." He tacked on the name to reestablish in his mind who she was.

"I can't account for that."

"Try."

"I *can't*," she said, her voice cracking.

He crouched down in front of her, and caught himself about to place his hands on her knees. They were face-to-face now, inches apart. From this close, he should be able to detect any artifice. *Should* be able to.

"Judge Cato Laird wants you dead."

"Yes."

"He's a rich and powerful man."

"That doesn't exclude him from wanting to have me killed."

"But he hires a bargain-basement assassin to do it?" He shook his head with skepticism.

"I know it sounds implausible, but I swear to you it's true."

He searched her eyes for signs of drug-induced paranoia or hallucination. None there.

Her husband doted on her, so it was unlikely that she was trying to spice up her mundane existence by creating some excitement.

Schizophrenia? Possibly. Compulsive liar? Maybe.

There was also a chance she was telling the truth, but the odds of that were so slim as to be negligible. Knowing Cato Laird, knowing Gary Ray Trotter, it just didn't gel.

What Duncan suspected, what he believed with every instinct

that had made him a good detective, was that she was trying to cover her own sweet ass, and that, because of what he'd said to her the night of the awards dinner, she was trying to use him to do it.

Why her sweet ass needed covering, he didn't know yet. But, based on what he and DeeDee had discovered last night at Meyer Napoli's office, he would soon find out. In the meantime, it pissed him off that she thought he'd be that easily manipulated, and he wanted to tell her so.

For the moment, however, he would continue to play along. "Implausible is precisely the word I would use, Mrs. Laird. I can't wrap my mind around the idea of the judge contracting with someone as inept as Trotter."

"All I know is this. If I hadn't fired the pistol when I did—and I did *not* fire first, no matter how many theories to the contrary you parade out—I would be dead. Cato would have told this story about a burglar caught in the act, and who wouldn't believe him?"

She stood up so suddenly she almost knocked Duncan over. "He's a superior court judge. He's from a wealthy, influential family. It would never occur to anyone that he would hire someone to kill his wife."

"It certainly would never occur to me."

His inflection brought her around slowly to face him.

He shrugged his shoulders. "I mean, he would have to be crazy, wouldn't he?"

"What do you mean?"

"Come on," he said, his voice as taunting as his smile. "What man in his right mind would want to get rid of a wife like you?"

She regarded him closely for several long moments, then said softly, with defeat, "You don't believe me."

His smile vanished and his tone turned harsh. "Not a goddamn word."

"Why?" Her voice had gone thin. If he didn't know better, he would swear she was genuinely perplexed.

To keep himself from falling for it, he gave a sardonic snuffle. "The judge has got himself a live-in topless waitress."

She took a deep breath, the defeat settling on her even more heavily. "Oh."

"Yeah. Oh."

"Because I worked topless, I'm automatically a liar, is that it?"

"Not at all. But it doesn't particularly lend credence to your story, does it. I mean, the judge can look his fill, touch his fill, screw his fill, and he doesn't have to tip. You're every man's wet dream."

She continued to stare at him for several beats, her hurt and bafflement rapidly turning to anger. "You're cruel, Detective."

"I get that a lot. Especially from people who I know are lying to me."

She turned her back to him and marched toward the door. He crossed the room in three long strides and caught her as she was fumbling with the latch. He grabbed her by the shoulders and brought her around.

"Why'd you come here?"

"I told you!"

"The judge hired Trotter to kill you."

"Yes!"

"Bullshit! I've seen him with you. He can't keep his hands off you."

She tried to wrestle herself free of his grasp, but he wouldn't let her.

"You're his prized possession, Mrs. Laird. That six-carat marquise diamond on your left hand took you off the market and bought him whirlpool baths and second helpings in bed. And it's all legal, tied up neat and proper with a marriage license. Now, why would he want you dead?"

She remained silent, glaring up at him.

"*Why?* If I'm to believe this sob story, I've got to hear a motive. Give me one."

"I can't!"

"Because there isn't one."

"There is, but I can't risk telling you. Not . . . not now."

"Why?"

"Because you wouldn't believe me."

"I might."

"You haven't believed anything else."

"That's right. I haven't. Cato Laird has no motive whatsoever to kill you. You, on the other hand, have an excellent motive for coming here and trying to win me to your side."

"What are you talking about?"

"You don't want me to learn the truth of what went down that night."

"I—"

"Who was Trotter to you?"

"No one. I'd never seen him before."

"Oh, I think you had. I think you knew who was waiting for you in the study, and that's why instead of calling 911, you armed yourself with a loaded pistol, which, by the way, you knew how to fire with deadly accuracy."

He lowered his face close to hers and said in a stage whisper, "I'm this close to booking you for murder." That wasn't true, but he wanted to see what kind of reaction he would get.

It was drastic. She went very still, very pale, and looked very afraid.

"Well, I see that got your attention," he said. "Do you want to change your story now?"

She redoubled her efforts to break his hold. "Coming here was a mistake."

"You're damn right it was."

"I was wrong about you. I thought you would believe me."

"No, what you thought was that if you showed up at my place looking as inviting as an unmade bed, I'd forget all about poor old Gary Ray Trotter. And if one thing led to another and we wound up in the sack, I might drop the investigation of that shooting altogether."

Furious now, she pushed hard against his chest. "Let go of me."

He shook her slightly, demanding, "Isn't that the reason for this secret meeting?"

"No!"

"Then tell me what possible motive Cato Laird could have for wanting to kill you."

"You wouldn't believe me."

"Try me."

"I already did!"

She practically flung the words into his face and met his hot gaze with one equally fierce. Neither of them was moving now, except for the rise and fall of her chest against his. He was dangerously aware of that, damnably aware of every point at which they were touching.

"The only reason I came here was in the hope of convincing you that my husband is going to kill me." Her voice was gruff with emotion, vibrating through her body into his. "And because you don't believe me, he'll do it. What's more, he'll get away with it."

CHAPTER
9

"His second tee time was at eleven ten," DeeDee said as she tossed several Goldfish into her mouth.

She and Duncan were in the bar of the Silver Tide Country Club. It was crowded on this Saturday afternoon. Ralph Lauren's summer line was well represented. Duncan felt conspicuous in his sport jacket, but his shoulder holster and nine-millimeter would have made him even more so.

Among the drinkers were local political figures, private-practice physicians, real estate developers who made a killing off snowbirds who migrated by the thousands to the South's golf course communities each winter, and Stan Adams, the defense attorney who represented a coterie of career criminals, the most notable being Robert Savich. Adams did a double take when DeeDee and Duncan strolled in, then studiously pretended they didn't exist.

Which was just as well, Duncan thought. In his present mood, he wouldn't trust his temper if the lawyer had goaded him about his famous client. Although Savich had kept a low profile since the mistrial, not for a moment did Duncan think he was on hiatus from his criminal activity. He was just smart enough to exercise extreme caution till things cooled down.

Duncan also figured that he was plotting the best time and most effective way to strike at him. He knew Savich would. He'd practically promised it that day in the courtroom. It was only a matter of time before he did. Unfortunately, as a law officer, Duncan couldn't go after Savich without provocation. He had to sit and wait and wonder. That probably tickled Savich no end.

After seeing their badges, the Silver Tide's bartender had served him and DeeDee their drinks gratis. The bar had a nice ambience—dark wood, potted jungle plants, brass lamps, peppy but unobtrusive music. The lemonade Duncan had ordered was hand squeezed. The air conditioner was sufficient to keep the heat and humidity on the other side of the oversized, tinted windows. The view of the emerald golf course was spectacular. It wasn't a bad place in which to spend a sweltering afternoon.

Duncan would rather be anywhere else.

DeeDee dusted Goldfish crumbs off her fingers, remarking, "That must be Mrs. Laird's replacement."

She nodded toward the attractive young woman who was delivering a tray of drinks to a foursome of middle-aged men. They stopped discussing their golf game long enough to ogle and flirt.

"She and the judge have been married nearly three years," Duncan said. "Isn't that what you told me? The club's probably gone through a dozen or so waitresses since Mrs. Laird worked here."

DeeDee turned toward the doorway as another group of men wandered in. Cato Laird wasn't among them. "He played two rounds back to back, starting before seven this morning. If you can believe anybody would voluntarily do that."

"You'd have to hold a gun to my head."

"You don't like golf?"

"Too slow. Too passive. Not enough action."

"Playing piano isn't exactly an action sport."

"I don't play piano."

"Right." She consulted her wristwatch. "The guy at the desk said he should be finishing soon."

At least Elise hadn't been lying about her husband's tee time. She'd said he had an early one.

She'd said a lot of things.

The last thing she'd said was that her husband was going to kill her, and that when he did he would get away with it, and that it would be Duncan's fault because he hadn't believed her.

Then she had squirmed out of his grasp, and with a slam of the front door she was outta there. Her squirming had left him with a doomed erection and respiration more labored than it had been during his five-mile run through the syrupy dawn air. He'd been so angry and frustrated—at her for roping him into her little drama, at himself for allowing her to—he'd actually banged his fist against his front door.

It still hurt. He flexed and contracted his fingers now in an attempt to ease the throbbing ache.

After that burst of temper, he'd gulped a two-liter bottle of water while standing in a cold shower, which had reduced his sweating and deflated his hopeful but disappointed dick. Then he'd called DeeDee as promised.

She had arrived at his town house at the appointed time, bringing with her a selection of breakfast muffins and two cups of carry-out coffee, because, as she said, "Yours sucks."

She had a plan mapped out for the day. Grouchily, he had reminded her that he was the senior member of the team, the men*tor*. "You're the men*tee*."

"You want to pull rank, fine. What do you think we should do?"

"I think we should confront the judge with what we learned last night. I'm anxious to see his reaction."

"That's what I just said."

"That's why I agreed to let you be my partner. You're smart." Rummaging in the carry-out sack, he frowned. "Didn't you get any blueberry?"

He kept up the familiar, squabbling repartee on purpose, because all the while they were in the town house, he'd been afraid that DeeDee would sense that Elise had been there. The moment he'd admitted his partner through the front door, he'd expected her to stop in her tracks and say, "Has Elise Laird been here?" Because to him, the essence of her was that powerful and pervasive. He could feel it, smell it, taste it.

Halfway through his second muffin, he suggested that DeeDee call the Silver Tide Country Club.

"How come?"

"It's Saturday. I have a hunch the judge is playing golf."

DeeDee's call to the club confirmed what Elise had told him. DeeDee was informed that the judge was playing his second round. Their plan was to be waiting for him when he finished, catch him relaxed and unaware, spring on him what they'd learned last night, and gauge his reaction.

They'd been waiting now for more than half an hour. Duncan was about to order another lemonade for lack of anything better to do when the bartender approached them. "The front desk just called, said to tell y'all Judge Laird is having lunch on the terrace."

He pointed them through a pair of French doors at one end of the bar that opened onto a loggia. At least that's what the bartender called the open-air walkway enshrouded by leafy wisteria vine. "It'll lead you straight to the dining terrace."

"I hope it's shaded," Duncan muttered.

The tables set up on the terrace were indeed shaded by white umbrellas as large as parachutes, trimmed in braided cotton fringe. Each table had a pot of vibrant pink geraniums in its center. The judge was seated at one, a cloth napkin folded over his linen trousers, a glass of what looked like scotch at his place setting.

He stood up as they approached. They'd been notified that he was on the terrace, but he'd also been notified that the detectives had been waiting on him in the bar. He wasn't surprised to see them, but he didn't appear to be particularly perturbed either.

Of course, he had an audience. Duncan was aware of curious glances cast at them by other diners as the judge shook hands with him and DeeDee in turn and offered them seats at the table.

"I'm about to have lunch. I hope you'll join me."

"No, thank you," DeeDee said. "We had a late breakfast."

"A drink at least." He signaled a waiter, who hastened over. DeeDee ordered a Diet Coke. Duncan switched to iced tea.

"How was your game? Games?" DeeDee amended herself, giving the judge her best smile. The women around her were in sundresses and halter tops, showing off well-tended tans and pedicured toenails. If she was self-conscious of her dark, tailored suit and sensible walking shoes, she gave no outward sign of it. Duncan admired her for that.

The judge modestly admitted to an eighty on the first round, an eighty-four on the second. While she was commending him, he noticed Duncan whisking a bead of sweat off his forehead.

"I realize it's warm out here, Detective Hatcher." He smiled apologetically. "I defer to my wife, who sometimes gets cold in air-conditioning. She prefers the terrace to the sixty-degree thermostat inside."

Duncan was about to point out the obvious—that his wife wasn't there—when he experienced a sinking sensation in his gut that coincided with the judge's brightening smile. "There she is now."

He stood up, tossed his napkin onto the table, and went to meet Elise as she followed a hostess toward the table. Cato Laird embraced her. She removed her sunglasses to return his hug, and over her husband's shoulder she spotted Duncan, standing beside his chair at the table, not even realizing that he'd stood up.

Her eyes widened fractionally, but they shifted away from him so quickly that he thought he might have imagined it. As soon as the judge released her, she replaced her dark glasses.

She was dressed in dazzling white, as though to color-coordinate herself with the umbrellas. It was a simple, sleeveless blouse and a loose skirt. The outfit was tasteful. Correct. Unrevealing.

So why did his mind immediately venture to what was underneath?

He felt like he'd just sustained a kick in the balls. For the second time that morning, the unexpected appearance of Elise Laird had left him feeling untethered, which was an alien emotion for him.

Up till now, his involvements with women were dependent on his mood, his level of interest, and time available. The women's interest was usually guaranteed. He never took undue advantage of his appeal, and had even managed to remain friendly with most of his former girlfriends. On the rare occasion that his interest wasn't reciprocated, he took it in stride and didn't look back. No woman had ever broken his heart.

He'd proposed marriage only once: to a childhood friend with whom he remained very close. The catalyst had been the celebration of his thirty-fifth birthday. He pointed out to his friend that they weren't getting any younger, that both of them had remained single for a reason, and that maybe the reason was that they should be married to each other. He took her "Are you *nuts?*" as a no, and came to realize what she already knew. They loved each other dearly, but they weren't in love.

He'd had more women than some men. Much fewer than others. But *never* a principal in an investigation. And *never* a married woman. Elise Laird was both. Which made this uncommonly strong attraction to her not only unfortunate but absolutely forbidden.

Tell that to his tingling sensors.

The judge escorted her to the table and held her chair. He sat down and replaced his napkin in his lap, then secured his wife's hand, holding it clasped between both of his. "I called Elise and asked if she would like to join me for lunch. I thought it would be good for her to get out." He smiled at her affectionately.

"Obviously I thought so, too. Thank you for the invitation." She returned his smile, then looked across the pot of geraniums at DeeDee. "Hello, Detective Bowen."

"We hate to bust in on your lunch date, Mrs. Laird. But I suppose it's just as well you're here, too. We were about to tell the judge about the latest development."

Elise turned quickly to Duncan. "What development?"

"Something that came up last night." As he said the words, he realized he was assuring her that he hadn't told DeeDee about her visit to his town house. Her evident relief didn't make him feel any better about it.

The waiter arrived with his and DeeDee's drinks, along with a lemonade for Elise. It was like the one he'd had at the bar, except that hers was served with a strawberry as big as an apple impaled on a clear plastic skewer.

The judge ordered another scotch. The waiter asked if they'd like to see menus, but the judge said he would let him know when they were ready. DeeDee requested a straw, and the waiter apologized profusely for not bringing one. These distractions allowed Duncan and Elise time to exchange a long look. At least she was looking toward him. He couldn't see her eyes through the dark shades.

Trickles of sweat were rolling down his torso, and it wasn't only because of the heat. The tension at the table was palpable. Even though they were all going through the motions of being relaxed in one another's company, pretending that this was a casual gathering without agenda, they all knew better.

No one said anything until DeeDee's straw had been delivered. She thanked the waiter with a nod, peeled away the wrapper, and stuck the straw in her glass. "Judge Laird, are you familiar with Meyer Napoli?"

He laughed. "Of course. He's been in my courtroom too many times to count."

"As a defendant?" DeeDee asked.

"Only as a witness," the judge replied unflappably.

"For which side?"

"Depending on the case, he's testified both for the prosecution and the defense."

"Who is he?"

"Sorry, darling." The judge turned to Elise. "Meyer Napoli is a private investigator."

"Had you never heard of him, Mrs. Laird?"

Elise removed her sunglasses and gave DeeDee a level look. "If I had, I wouldn't have asked."

A crease had formed between the judge's eyebrows. "You mentioned a development."

The judge addressed the statement to Duncan, so he responded. "Meyer Napoli has gone missing. It became official this morning. It's been over twenty-four hours since anyone has seen or heard from him. His secretary, who seems to be the person closest to him, is convinced that he's met with foul play."

The judge was hanging on every word. When Duncan stopped with that, he raised his shoulders in a slight shrug. "I hate to hear that. I hope the secretary is wrong, but how does this relate to us? What possible bearing could a private investigator's disappearance have to do with what happened in our home night before last?"

Duncan locked gazes with Elise. "We found Gary Ray Trotter's name among papers on Napoli's desk."

Her lips parted slightly, but Duncan didn't expect her to say anything and she didn't. In fact, no one spoke for a noticeable length of time.

Finally DeeDee cleared her throat. "The detective investigating Napoli's disappearance noticed Trotter's name on a memo. Actually a personalized Post-it. 'From the desk of Meyer Napoli.' The detective thought it coincidental, Trotter being recently . . . deceased. He knew that Detective Hatcher and I would find that interesting, and he was right. We talked to Napoli's secretary last night."

"And?" the judge asked.

"And nothing," DeeDee replied. "Trotter had never made an appointment with the secretary to see Napoli. She doesn't remember anybody by that name coming to the office, but, of course, that doesn't mean that Trotter and Napoli didn't meet somewhere else. Obviously they did. Or had contact of some kind, because the secretary confirmed that the handwriting on the Post-it was Napoli's." She looked back and forth between the judge and Elise.

The judge chuckled. "You've thrown out a lot of assumptions, Detective. Any one of which could be fact. Or none of them. Perhaps Napoli heard through the grapevine that Trotter had died during the commission of a crime. His name rang a bell and Napoli jotted it down to remind himself of it later. Who knows where their paths crossed? Maybe Trotter owed him money." He gave her a gentle, somewhat patronizing smile. "Aren't those as plausible as your assumptions?"

Duncan wouldn't have been surprised if DeeDee had launched herself across the table and knocked him on his condescending ass. He wouldn't have blamed her, either.

Instead she gave the judge an abashed grin. "Detective Hatcher chides me constantly for jumping to conclusions. It's one of my character flaws. However, this time he agrees with me."

The judge looked toward Duncan for elaboration. Duncan nodded him back toward DeeDee, indicating that she still had the floor.

She said, "Meyer Napoli has questionable ethics, but he's reputed to have a mind like a steel trap. He wouldn't need to jot himself a reminder note. He wrote down Gary Ray Trotter's name for a reason."

Elise had been following this exchange silently, but with undivided attention. "Are you implying that . . ." Then she shook her head in confusion and asked, "What are you implying?"

"I think I can answer that, darling," the judge said. "They're implying that there's a connection between Napoli and Trotter, and by association, between Napoli and us. Is that it, Detective Bowen?"

In view of his testiness, she responded with remarkable calm. "We're not implying anything, Judge Laird. But it struck us as coincidental that less than twenty-four hours after he was fatally shot in your home, Trotter's name would show up on the desk of a private investigator who, also coincidentally, has been reported missing. It's strange, to say the least."

"I'm sorry. I can't explain the strangeness of it."

DeeDee continued with her typical doggedness. "Please try, Judge Laird. If there was a connection, no matter how long ago or how remote, it might explain how Trotter chose your house to break into. It seems far-fetched that he chose it at random. That's a quirky element of this case we just can't reconcile. Why did he choose you to burglarize?"

"Unfortunately, Mr. Trotter is in no position to tell us, so I doubt we'll ever know," he said. "He could have heard of us through Napoli, I suppose, if they had a history, even in passing. Beyond that, I can't venture a guess."

"You've never had direct contact with Napoli?"

"Not outside my courtroom. My wife had never even heard of him until a few minutes ago."

"Is that right, Mrs. Laird?"

"That's right. I'd never heard of Napoli. Nor Trotter."

DeeDee sucked the last of her Coke through the straw. "Then I guess we've wasted your time. Thanks for the Coke." She reached for her handbag, and the judge took that as a signal that the interview was over.

"They make an excellent shrimp salad," he said. "I'd be pleased to treat you."

DeeDee thanked him for the offer but declined. The judge stood up and shook hands with each of them. DeeDee smiled down at Elise and told her good-bye.

Duncan was about to walk past Elise's chair, when he hesitated, then extended his hand to her, almost as a dare to himself. First of all, it's not easy to shake hands with a woman who's given you a hard-on, and knows it. And second, he was thinking about what had happened the last time they shook hands. "Good-bye, Mrs. Laird."

She hesitated, then took his hand. Or did she *clutch* it? "Good-bye."

It was more difficult to pull his eyes away from hers than it was to withdraw his hand. He followed DeeDee inside the clubhouse and through the dining room. They waited to speak until they reached the lobby and she had given the parking valet her claim check. "What do you think?"

Before Duncan could answer, Stan Adams strolled up to them. "Well, Detective Sergeant Hatcher, I see that you and Judge Laird have kissed and made up since Savich's trial." He grinned at Duncan, then greeted DeeDee.

"Is this what you do in your spare time?" she asked. "You hang out in the country club until Savich commits another murder?"

The lawyer laughed, but became serious when he turned back to Duncan. "Are you investigating the fatal shooting at the judge's house the other night? What was the guy's name, Trotter?"

Duncan wasn't surprised that Adams knew of the incident. As DeeDee's society friend had said, the story had created a buzz. It also had been reported in the newspaper. Subtly. The judge, who usually basked in the glow of media attention, must have called in a favor with the managing editor.

The story had been buried on page ten and details were practically nonexistent. According to the brief story, Trotter was an intruder who had made an attempt on Mrs. Laird's life, then later died. He could have died of a heart attack or cholera for all the reading public knew.

Stan Adams said, "I thought it was self-defense. How come y'all are on it?"

"Like you, we're always trying to drum up business." Duncan's grin was as affable as the attorney's, but equally insincere.

Adams knew he would get no more information from them. "Well, if it turns out that Mrs. Laird needs a good defense lawyer, I hope you'll recommend me."

He walked away and had reached the double entrance doors, when DeeDee called out to him. "Oh, Mr. Adams, I just remembered. Your dentist called. It's time you had them bleached again." She tapped her front teeth.

The attorney fired a finger pistol at her and said, "Good one, Detective. Good one."

Then he was gone. DeeDee muttered under her breath, "Asshole. Every time I think of that mistrial . . ." She made a snarling sound and clenched her fist.

Duncan was looking at her, but not really seeing her. His mind wasn't on Savich or his oily attorney. It was on the judge. His cream-colored linen trousers, his cool and courteous manner.

"A drink at least. . . . They make an excellent shrimp salad."

He hadn't even broken a sweat.

"Here's the car," DeeDee said and started for the door. Realizing he wasn't following, she turned back. "Duncan?"

But his mind was still on the judge. Tucking his wife's hand into the crook of his elbow. Possessively.

"Tell me what possible motive Cato Laird could have for wanting to kill you."

"You wouldn't believe me."

Making a split-second decision, Duncan told DeeDee to go on ahead. "I'm going to stick around here for a while."

CHAPTER
10

J UDGE AND MRS. LAIRD TOOK THEIR TIME OVER LUNCH. DUNCAN had been spying for—he checked his wristwatch—one hour and twelve minutes.

DeeDee had argued against leaving, reminding him that if she did, he would be on foot. He said he would call a taxi and insisted that she return to the Barracks and see if they'd received the ballistics reports on the two weapons fired in the Lairds' house.

Primarily they'd been interested to learn if Trotter's pistol had been used in the commission of another crime, but had decided, what the hell, while they were at it, it wouldn't hurt also to test the one Elise Laird had fired.

Duncan had also asked DeeDee to check with Kong for any updates on the missing Meyer Napoli. "If Kong's not in today, call his cell phone." It was possible that the PI's secretary was wrong and that her boss was shacked up with a new girlfriend. If so, this case, and by extension Duncan's life, would be made simpler.

After seeing DeeDee off, Duncan returned to the country club's casual dining room and claimed a table that provided an unobstructed view of the Lairds' table on the terrace. The judge had ordered a roast beef sandwich, Elise the recommended shrimp salad. Two parties had stopped at their table to chat briefly, but their exchanges had been mostly with the judge.

There were few lapses in the Lairds' conversation with each other, and both seemed totally absorbed in it. After they finished the meal and were waiting for their plates to be removed, he stroked her bare arm from shoulder to elbow, and once he raised her hand to his mouth and kissed the palm of it.

For the whole seventy-two minutes that Duncan had been observing them, he saw nothing to indicate that the judge wanted her dead. Instead, Cato Laird seemed like a man totally besotted with a woman that he might want to fuck to death, but otherwise had no intention of killing.

When the judge signaled for the check, Elise excused herself and left the table. She didn't see Duncan when she passed through the dining room in which he was seated. He got up and followed into an empty hallway, and saw her go into the ladies' room.

He waited, he paced, keeping a nervous eye on the terrace. The judge signed the tab, pocketed his receipt, and left the table. "Shit!" Duncan hissed. But, fortunately for him, before the judge reached the door, a group of men at another table hailed him and he stopped to chat. Duncan hoped they had a lot of breeze to shoot.

Sensing movement behind him, he turned. When Elise saw him she drew up short, half in, half out the door.

"Trying to decide whether to brave it or slink back into the powder room?"

She stepped into the hallway and let the door close behind her. "I thought you'd left."

"And I thought you might have changed your mind."

"About what?"

"That crock of crap you told me this morning."

"It's the truth."

"Now, now. Is that any way to talk about your husband after he treated you to that romantic lunch?" Her eyes flashed angrily. She tried to sidestep him, but he didn't let her, saying, "I caught your trick with the cherry."

For dessert, both she and the judge had ordered iced coffee drinks with whipped cream on top. The judge had offered his to her.

"I watched you lean in and pull that cherry off the stem with your lips. And I gotta tell you, Mrs. Laird, it was sexy as all get-out.

The kind of come-on a man can't mistake. Even with a tinted window between us, I got aroused."

"I have to act as though everything is normal."

"You normally do things for him like sucking that fruit into your mouth?" He snuffled a laugh. "That bastard's got all the luck."

Color spread up from her chest into her cheeks. Whether the blush was from embarrassment or anger, he didn't know, but he suspected she was getting angrier by the moment. She barely moved her lips, pushing the words through her teeth. "Don't you understand? If I tip my hand, I'll be dead."

"Hmm. Okay. Makes sense. And the reason your husband wants you dead is . . . why?"

She remained silent.

"Oh, right." He snapped his fingers. "He's got no motive."

"He has motive."

Duncan moved closer, lowered his volume, but increased the intensity of his voice. "Then tell me what it is."

"I can't!" She looked beyond his shoulder, registering alarm. "Cato."

He turned to see Laird entering the dining room. He spotted them immediately. Coming back around to Elise, Duncan said, "You know, I could just ask him if he wants you dead and why."

He'd tossed that out there just to see her reaction.

Her face drained of the color that had filled it only moments before. The fear looked genuine. Either that, or she was very good.

No. Please.

Reading the soundless words on her lips worked more effectively than if she'd spoken them aloud.

"Detective Hatcher, I thought you'd left hours ago." As he joined them, the judge was smiling, but Duncan could tell that he wasn't pleased to see him. He divided a curious look between him and Elise. "You seemed awfully engrossed in your conversation."

She said, "I bumped into him on my way out of the restroom."

"And I told Mrs. Laird that I needed to talk to you. Alone." Out the corner of his eye, he watched Elise. He saw her breath catch.

"I'm scheduled for a massage," the judge said. "You can follow me to the locker room and talk to me while I change."

"Downstairs?" The judge nodded. "I'll wait for you there. Mrs. Laird."

Duncan looked directly into her eyes, then turned away.

The judge came into the locker room a few minutes later. "She's still not herself," he said without preamble. "On edge. Jittery. I think it will take a while for her to recover from this."

"It was frightening."

"And then some. My locker's over here." He led Duncan down a row of lockers and when he reached his, he began working the combination lock.

Duncan sat down on a padded bench nearby. "Before I forget, I charged my lunch to your account. Club sandwich and iced tea. You know they charge for refills? I also added a twenty-five percent gratuity."

"Twenty-five percent? Very generous of you."

"I figured you would have a soft spot for the waitstaff here."

The judge gave him a wry look. "You've done some background investigation."

"That's my job."

"So you know Elise's employment history. I suppose you also know what she did before she came to work here at the club." He stated it, he didn't ask. "Do you think less of her for it?"

"No. Do you?"

Duncan's brusque comeback got the judge's ire up. The heavy lock thumped against the blond wood locker when he let go of it. Angrily, he turned toward Duncan. Then, rather than take issue, the fight went out of him. He sat down on the far end of the bench.

He shook his head with self-deprecation. "I'm a cliché, I suppose. Actually, I *know* I am. I knew I would be when I began seeing Elise, not just here at the club, but actually taking her out."

"Sleeping with her."

The judge raised one shoulder in a negligent shrug. "Gossip spread like wildfire among my friends and associates. Our affair became the talk of this club. Then of all Savannah. Or so it seemed."

"That didn't bother you?"

"No, because I was in love. Still am. As much as possible I ignored the gossip. Then a 'well-meaning friend,' " he said, forming quotation marks with his fingers, "invited me to lunch one day for the express purpose of informing me that the cocktail waitress I was seeing wasn't a suitable companion for a man of my position and social standing. He told me where she'd worked before the Silver Tide. He expected me to be shocked, horrified. But I already knew about Elise's former employment."

"You'd done your own investigating."

"No, Elise had told me herself. She was honest about it from the start, which made me love her all the more. Acquaintances of mine who overtly snubbed her, I consider *former* friends. Who needs friends like that? But it bothers Elise. She thinks I've suffered because of our marriage."

"Have you?"

"Hardly."

"You haven't run for reelection since you married her. Voters may side with those former friends of yours."

"I'm sure anyone running against me will dredge up her past. We're prepared for that. We'll own up to it and dismiss it as irrelevant, and it is."

"Except that it may cost you the election. Will you be okay with that?"

"Which would you choose, Detective? A judgeship, or Elise in your bed every night?"

Duncan realized he was being tested. He held the judge's stare for several beats, then deadpanned, "What's the choice?"

The judge laughed. "My feeling exactly." He raised his hands, palms up. "In the eyes of many, I'm a man to be pitied, a fool for love. I fell in love the moment I saw her, and I'm still in love."

Duncan stretched his feet far out in front of him and studied the toes of his shoes. "I believe that." He waited several seconds, then said, "What I don't believe is that you had no dealings with Meyer Napoli except inside your courtroom." He gave up the study of his footwear and turned his head. "You lied about that, Judge."

Duncan won the staring contest. The initial challenge in the judge's glare slowly evaporated. Finally he sighed with resignation. "You're good, Detective."

"Thanks, but I don't need your compliments. I need an explanation for why you lied."

He took a deep breath, let it out slowly. "So Elise would never know that I had hired Meyer Napoli to follow her."

Duncan had thought it might be something like that. "Why did you?"

"I'm not proud of it."

"That's not what I asked."

"I can't believe I resorted to hiring that—"

"Unscrupulous sleazoid," Duncan said, impatient because he wasn't getting a straight answer. "Napoli didn't come with character references, but you hired him anyway. You hired him to follow your wife. Why?"

"Again, it's a cliché. The oldest reason in the world." He looked sadly at Duncan.

"She was having an affair."

The judge's vulnerable smile was out of character for the man Duncan knew, but he supposed a cuckold was about as humble a creature as there was. "I had my suspicions," he replied. "But before I tell you anything more, I want you to understand that it happened months ago. Last year."

"Okay."

"It's over and has been for some time," he insisted.

"Okay."

Satisfied that he'd made that crucial point, the judge said, "For months I tried to ignore the signs."

"She had a headache every night?"

He chuckled. "No. Even at the height of my suspicion, Elise was as passionate in bed as she'd always been. Our sexual appetite for each other never waned."

Duncan tried to keep his expression impassive, but even if he couldn't, the judge wouldn't have noticed. He was submerged in his recollections.

"It was other things," he said. "Classic signs. Telephone calls she pretended were wrong numbers. Rushing in late for meals without having a good excuse for her lateness. Time unaccounted for."

"Sounds like an affair to me." Duncan was perversely glad to cast doubt on Cato Laird's confidence in his wife's sexual appetite for him.

"I thought so, too. It got so that the thought of her in bed with another man dominated my mind. It's all I could think about. If it was true, I had to know it, and I had to know who he was."

"So you retained the services of Meyer Napoli."

"Which indicates the degree of my desperation. I refused to go to his office. We met late one evening at a driving range. I practiced my swing while he asked pertinent questions. Did I know who her lover was? How long had the affair been going on?"

He shook his head with disgust. "I couldn't believe I was discussing my wife with a man of his caliber. His phraseology, the vulgar terms he used, I couldn't even apply to Elise. It all seemed so wrong, I started to call the whole thing off right then.

"But," he continued with a sigh, "I'd gone that far, and not knowing was making me miserable. So I gave him the required advance on his fee, and left. That's the last time I ever saw him."

Duncan had been following the story, practically anticipating every word the judge was going to say before he said it. It was a familiar story that he'd heard many times over the course of his career. Passion led to possessiveness and jealousy, which spawned all sorts of mayhem, and frequently murder.

But the judge's last statement didn't gibe with the rest of it. "The last time you ever saw him? Napoli didn't come through?"

"No, he came through," the judge said tightly.

"She *was* having an affair?"

"I don't know."

"Sorry, Judge. You've lost me."

"Napoli got back to me," he explained. "He had followed Elise to several clandestine meetings. He identified the man. He had times and places. But . . . but I stopped him there. I didn't want to hear any more. I didn't want it confirmed to me that she was having an affair."

"That's not the usual reaction, Judge," Duncan said slowly. "The husband may be the last to know, but he usually *wants* to know."

"Knowing wouldn't have made a difference in how much I loved her. I wouldn't have left her."

But would you want to kill her over it? Duncan thought. "So you never knew the details of those clandestine meetings?"

Looking pained, the judge shook his head. "No."

"Did she ever know you'd found her out?"

"No. I didn't want her to know I'd stooped so low as to have her spied on. I was ashamed of it. Besides, a few weeks after I dismissed Napoli, it ceased to matter."

Duncan frowned with misapprehension. "She stopped seeing the guy?"

"In a manner of speaking." After a beat, he said, "Elise's rendezvous were with Coleman Greer."

Even at midafternoon, the White Tie and Tails Club was as dark as midnight except for the strobes flashing on the girl dancing onstage, and the pink and blue neon stars that twinkled on the ceiling.

Well ahead of the Saturday night crowd that would pack the place after nightfall, a handful of customers were seated along the semicircular stage, nursing drinks and enjoying the dancer's performance. Only one was whistling and rowdily applauding the act.

Savich occupied a booth at the rear of the club, far enough from the stage that he could tolerate the volume of the music. He was seated on the banquette against the wall, facing out into the room. He never left his back exposed.

He watched as a hostess in black leather bra and chaps escorted Elise through the maze of empty tables and chairs. When they reached the booth, he indicated that Elise sit down.

"Can I bring you anything, Mr. Savich?" the hostess asked.

He looked at Elise inquisitively. She shook her head. "Are you sure?" he asked. "Pardon my saying so, but you look a bit strung out, like you could use a drink."

"No, thank you."

He waved the hostess off. "We're not to be disturbed."

As she walked away, she put an extra jiggle into her bare buttocks. "She's new. Trying to work her way up to dancer." With a smile, he returned his attention to Elise. "I'm sorry you had to come all this way. Kenny said you sounded urgent."

"Thank you for seeing me on such short notice."

"Speaking of short notice, you haven't given me much time, Elise. You must be in a bigger hurry than you indicated the other day."

"I am."

"Why? What's happened?"

"Nothing. Nothing else. I was just anxious to hear back from you."

He knew she was lying, but he let it pass. He rather enjoyed her vain effort to hide from him that a new development had upset her. Otherwise she wouldn't have called him on a Saturday afternoon, sounding "positively distraught," according to Kenny. She'd been so eager to see him, she had agreed to join him at the topless club where they'd first met. It was miles—and light-years—away from her home, her country club, her present life as Mrs. Cato Laird.

"How does it feel to be back in the White Tie and Tails?"

She took a cursory look around. "It seems like a long time ago since I worked here."

"You're still missed."

"I seriously doubt that. I've seen the new talent."

"But some girls leave a lasting impression." He let the words hover there between them for several moments. Then he leaned back against the padded banquette and reached for his gold cigarette case and lighter.

"Savich, were you able to—"

"Hatcher."

She flinched with surprise. Possibly with something else. "What about him?"

He took his time lighting his cigarette. "Is he still the detective on the case?"

"As of an hour ago."

"Duncan Hatcher, the *homicide* detective," he said. "Why does he continue to investigate the shooting?"

"He said there were loose ends that needed clearing up before he could close the case."

"And you believed that?" he asked, disdainful of her naivete. "He's digging, Elise. He's trying to find fault with your self-defense story."

"He's talking to us, that's all."

"You and your husband?"

"He's talking privately with Cato right now."

"Why privately?"

She took a deep breath, exhaled it along with the words "I don't know."

"Hmm. So that's what got you spooked."

"I'm not spooked."

Her short tone caused him to arch an eyebrow, reminding her that she had petitioned his help, and that she wasn't speaking to him with the deference that a petitioner should. It worked. She backed down.

"Were you able to do what I asked?" she said.

He blew a puff of smoke toward the ceiling. It swirled in the glow of the pink and blue neon stars. "Tell me, Elise, what do you think of Duncan Hatcher?"

"He's tough, just as you warned me he would be."

Lowering his voice, he said, "Maybe a more interesting question would be to ask what Detective Hatcher thinks of *you*, sweet Elise?"

"He thinks I'm a liar."

"Really?" Fixing his steady blue gaze on her, he idly stroked his cheek. "Are you?"

"No."

"Then you've got nothing to be afraid of."

"I'm afraid Detective Hatcher will continue to think I'm a liar."

"Change his mind," he said simply.

"I've tried. He didn't believe me."

"That doesn't surprise me. He can be charming. Or so I've heard. But under those rough-and-tumble Southern-boy, tawny good looks, he's all cop. A fucking cop," he said, letting his enmity toward Hatcher show.

"He won't close your case as long as there's one iota of doubt in his mind that it was self-defense. Hear me well, Elise. He'll leave no stone unturned. And he would delight in finding something nasty beneath one. There's bad blood between him and your husband."

"I know about that. Most recently they clashed over your mistrial."

"Yes, and for that, Hatcher would enjoy embarrassing you and the judge. Publicly if he can. But that's nothing compared to the plans he has for me. He's a man with a mission. He never forgets, and he never gives up."

"I sense that about him."

"You're in a dangerous spot, Elise."

She pulled her lower lip through her teeth. "He doesn't have any evidence to disprove self-defense."

"But Hatcher has been known to build cases out of virtually nothing, and, with the exception of my recent trial, he gets convictions and they stick despite appeals." Sounding almost mystified, he said, "The man actually believes in what he's doing. Right versus wrong. Good versus evil. He's a crusader. True blue. Seemingly incorruptible."

Snagged by his own words, he thought, *Seemingly* incorruptible.

Through the haze of cigarette smoke, he studied his guest. She really was a lovely girl. Classiness and sexiness in one stunning package. A tantalizing combination. Which even a crusader would find hard to resist.

The smile originated with his thoughts and spread slowly across his face. "Sweet Elise," he said, his voice dripping honey, "let's talk about this favor you asked of me. You'll be pleased to know I've already granted it."

CHAPTER
11

WHEN THE HIGH-PITCHED WARNING BEEP SIGNALED THAT A main door of the house had been opened, Elise swiftly left her bedroom. She'd reached the top of the stairs when she heard the chirps indicating that the code was being entered. Cato was home.

He appeared in the foyer below her. She called his name. He looked up and saw her poised there at the top of the staircase. "Hello, Elise. You're still awake. Why am I not surprised?" Rather than coming upstairs, he proceeded down the foyer, disappearing from her sight.

Her meeting with Savich had left her shaken. Meetings with Savich always did.

When she'd returned home, the house was empty. Mrs. Berry was off on Saturday evenings, so Elise hadn't expected to find her there. But it surprised her that Cato wasn't. As evening turned to night, she called his cell phone several times but got only his voice mail. He hadn't responded to her messages.

It was uncharacteristic of him not to keep in touch. It was also a bad omen. She passed the entire evening and into the wee hours in a state of high anxiety, wondering what Duncan Hatcher had told her husband.

She quickly descended the staircase. "Cato?"

"In here."

She followed the direction of his voice into the kitchen. As she entered, he turned to face her with a butcher knife in his hand. She looked from the gleaming blade to him. "What are you doing?"

"Making a sandwich." He moved aside, allowing her to see the ham on the countertop, along with fixings for a sandwich. "Would you like one?"

"No, thank you. Wouldn't you rather have breakfast? I could make—"

"This will do." He turned back to carving slices off the ham.

"I've been calling your cell phone all night. Where have you been?"

"Didn't you get the message?"

"No."

"I asked the receptionist at the club to call and tell you that I'd been invited into a high-stakes poker game and that it would be late before I got home."

He reached around her for the telephone, depressing the button that put it on speaker. The static dial tone indicated that no messages were waiting to be retrieved. "Hmm. That's odd. She's usually reliable."

Elise doubted he'd ever made the request to the receptionist. If he'd wanted to assuage her concern, why hadn't he just called her himself?

He built his sandwich and halved it with the butcher knife. "What time did you get home, Elise?"

"Around five, I think. After leaving you at the club, I got a call from the dress shop, telling me that my alterations were ready. I went to pick them up, did some shopping."

That much was the truth. But before going to the boutique where she often shopped, she'd driven to the edge of town to the White Tie and Tails Club to meet Robert Savich.

He put the sandwich on a plate and carried it to the table in the breakfast nook. "Buy anything?"

"A pants suit and a cocktail dress."

He licked a dollop of mayonnaise off his finger. "You can model them for me later."

"I think you'll approve." She sat down across from him, studying his expression, trying to make eye contact, which he was avoiding. "You've never stayed out all night before. Not once since we've been married."

He chewed a bite, blotted his mouth. "Not since we've been married have I had a day like yesterday."

He took another bite, chewed, blotted his mouth again. And he still wouldn't look at her. She was in an agony of suspense.

"My conversation with Duncan Hatcher was most upsetting."

Her throat closed.

"Even Kurt the massage Nazi couldn't work out the tension in my shoulders and back." He took another bite.

"What did he say to upset you? What did you talk about?"

"Our relationship. Yours and mine, not mine and his," he added, flashing a humorless smile.

"Our relationship is none of his business."

Then he did look at her directly. "Maybe he thinks it is."

"Why would he?"

"You tell me."

"I'm sorry, Cato. I don't know what you mean."

"Twice now I've come upon you two with your heads together, lost in conversation. The night of the awards dinner. And again today at the club. I didn't like it either time."

"The night of the awards dinner, he was a stranger asking me for change. Today, when I left the powder room, he was in the hallway, looking for you."

His dark eyes searched hers. "I wasn't that hard to find today. And he could have asked a dozen other people for change that night. He's deliberately putting himself in your path. You must sense why, Elise. You can't be that naive."

"You think Hatcher is interested in me romantically?"

He scoffed. "No romance about it. He'd love to sleep with you only to make a fool of me."

Cato had stayed away all night out of pique and jealousy. She felt her lungs expanding with relief.

"That would be the ultimate payback for my putting him in jail, wouldn't it?" he said. "To seduce my wife?"

Although Duncan Hatcher had said as much to her the night of the awards dinner, she smiled and shook her head. "You're wrong, Cato. He has no interest in me outside his investigation."

"What man could be immune to you?"

She smiled at the flattery.

"But what about you, Elise?"

"What about me?"

"What do you think of the detective?"

"You have to ask?" She placed her hand on his forearm where it rested on the table and squeezed it lightly. "Cato, since the night of the shooting, Detective Hatcher has done nothing but bully me. I dread the sight of him."

His features relaxed. "I'm glad to hear that." Pushing aside his plate, he reached across the table and stroked her cheek. "Let's get in the pool."

"Now? You just ate, and it's nearly dawn. Aren't you too tired to swim?"

"I'm wide awake. Apparently, so are you. And I didn't say I wanted to swim."

He took her hand and they walked outside together. She reached for the switch that turned on the pool light and the fountain in its center. He said, "No, leave them off."

He stripped to the skin. It was evident that he wasn't at all tired. He came to her, untied the belt of her robe, and pushed it off her, along with her slip-type nightgown. He ran his hands over her, possessively and with more aggressiveness than usual.

She responded as expected, but her mind was elsewhere. She was thinking of Duncan Hatcher. He hadn't betrayed her to Cato. Did that mean he believed her? Even a little?

Cato took her hand and pulled her down the steps into the pool. He clasped her around the waist and waded in until she could no longer touch bottom. As her body floated against his, she noticed that here in the center of the pool, the water was deep and dark. Like secrets.

"Duncan?"

He grunted a semblance of a response.

"That's yours."

"Hmm?" He lifted his head from the pillow and opened one eye.

"Your cell phone is ringing."

"Oh. Thanks." He rubbed sleep from his eyes with one hand and reached for his phone with the other. He flipped it open. "Yeah?"

"Guess who they hauled in last night and is still in a holding cell?"

"What time is it?" he grumbled, trying to pull the numbers of his alarm clock into focus.

"Gordon Ballew."

"Who?" How was it that DeeDee didn't sound groggy even on a Sunday morning?

"Gordie," she exclaimed. "Gordie Ballew. One of Savich's boys."

"Got it." With a groan, he rolled onto his back and sat up. The woman who'd been sleeping beside him was already up and across the room, gathering her clothing and pulling it on. "What did he do?"

"Who cares?" DeeDee said. "So long as we can get him in a bargaining mood. Meet you there."

She hung up before he could say anything more. He returned his cell phone to the nightstand and swung his feet to the floor. "Sorry, but I've got to run. Work."

"It's all right," she said as her head popped through the neck of her top. "I've got to go anyway."

He'd met her in one of the hot spots in Market Square last night. She was petite, pretty, and brunette. That was the sum total of what he knew about her. She'd told him some stuff, but the music had been loud, the drinks strong, and he hadn't really been listening anyway because he hadn't been that interested in anything she had to say.

He remembered none of their conversation, not even her name. He didn't specifically recall inviting her back to his place, but he must have. As for the act itself, the only thing he remembered was that he'd made sure to use a condom. Immediately after rolling off her, he'd fallen into a deep sleep.

It wasn't like him to bring home a stranger, but he'd thought that having sex, even mindless, meaningless sex, would keep him from thinking about Elise Laird.

Silly him.

His distraction must have made itself felt, and that was unfair to any woman. Feeling rotten about it, he said, "Look, you don't have to race out of here just because I do. Stay. Sleep. Make yourself at home. If this doesn't take too long, we could go out for breakfast later."

"No, thanks."

"Well, then, leave your number." He tried to inject his voice with a bit of enthusiasm, but was pretty sure he didn't achieve it. "I'd like to see you again."

"No, you wouldn't, but that's cool." She moved to the door, where she turned back and smiled. "You were a good fuck. Savich said you probably would be."

Gordon Ballew was one of those individuals who'd been doomed before he took his first breath. His mother hadn't been sure who his father was and didn't consider that it mattered much since she didn't keep the baby anyway.

Not even a barren couple desperate for an adopted child wanted one with a cleft palate, so from the delivery room Gordie had become a dependent of the state, shuttled from one foster home to another until he was old enough to exit the system and try and fare on his own.

His entire life had been an endless round of ridicule and abuse because of his deformed mouth, defective speech, and diminutive size. Today, at age thirty-three, he might weigh 120 pounds, sopping wet.

Duncan would have felt sorry for Gordie Ballew, except for the fact that he had never tried to improve his lot, had never attempted to reverse the downward spiral that his life had been since he wormed his way out of the birth canal.

Once he bade his last set of foster parents good-bye, he'd been in and out of penal institutions so many times that Duncan figured Gordie considered a cell block home.

He watched him thoughtfully on the video monitor in the room

adjacent to the interrogation room, where a member of the counter-
narcotics team had been hammering away at him for several hours,
without success.

"Has the DEA been notified?"

Another narcotics officer shook his head and gave a sour har-
rumph. "They've been such bastards, blaming us 'cause Freddy
Morris got popped, I figure we don't owe them this."

"*Did* we cause Freddy Morris to get popped?" Duncan asked.

"Hell no," the officer answered with soft but angry emphasis.

"Savich got him past you. All of you."

The officer grunted agreement without accepting blame. "I don't
see how he coulda done that."

"He couldn't," Duncan said. "Not without help."

The narc looked at him sharply. "From inside? Are you saying
somebody on our team ratted us out?"

It was a touchy subject, one that had been broached before to a
barrage of protests from both teams. It was something constantly
in the back of Duncan's mind, but he dropped it for now.

"Where's Ballew's lawyer?"

"Waived one," the narc told him. "Said he was ready to sign a
confession, go straight to jail, do not pass Go."

DeeDee had been practically dancing in place with impatience.
"Are we going to get a crack at him, or what?"

"Be our guest," the narc said.

As they moved toward the interrogation room, DeeDee asked
Duncan, "Were you good cop or bad cop last time we questioned
Gordie?"

"Bad. Let's stick with that."

"Okay."

The narc opened the door to the small, dreary room and told the
interrogating officer that he had a phone call. "Besides, homicide has
a hard-on for our boy here."

"Homicide?" Gordie squeaked.

The narcotics officer stepped aside to make room for Duncan
and DeeDee. "He's all yours. Y'all have fun." He strolled out and let
the door swing closed behind him.

"Hi, Gordie." DeeDee took a seat across the small table from him. "How are you?"

"How's it look?" he mumbled.

Ignoring the attitude behind his reply, she introduced herself by name. "Remember us? My partner there is Duncan Hatcher."

"I know you." Gordie cast a wary glance toward Duncan where he was leaning up against the wall, arms folded over his chest, ankles crossed.

"Didn't the narcs get you anything to drink? What would you like?" She moved as though to get up.

"Sit down, DeeDee," Duncan said. "He doesn't need anything to drink."

DeeDee frowned at him with feigned asperity and dropped back into the chair. "You picked the wrong time to get busted, Gordie. Duncan's pissed. He had plans for this morning, but now he's here with you."

"Don't let me keep you, Detective."

The con's cheeky courage was short-lived. He shriveled under Duncan's hard glare. "Let's stop screwing around," he said to DeeDee, "book him for murder two, and I can be on my way."

"The guy died?" Gordie squealed. "He wasn't bleeding that much. Swear to God it was an accident. I didn't mean to hurt him that bad. He said something about my lip. I was high. It happened before I realized. Oh Jesus. Murder two? I'll confess to assault, but . . . Oh Jesus."

"Relax, Gordie." Duncan's somber tone and the sinister way in which he pushed himself away from the wall and sauntered toward the table didn't inspire relaxation.

Gordie Ballew began to cry, his knobby shoulders bobbing up and down.

"Duncan, he needs a Kleenex," DeeDee said kindly.

"No, he doesn't." Duncan sat down on the corner of the table.

Gordie wiped his running nose on his sleeve and looked up at him with patent fear. "He *died?* I barely swiped him with that broken bottle."

"The guy you assaulted last night was treated and released."

Gordie sniffed loudly. He gaped up at Duncan, then looked at DeeDee, who nodded encouragingly. "Then how come y'all're talking murder two?"

"Another case, Gordie. Freddy Morris."

His face, flushed with anxiety moments before, turned pale. He licked snot off his misshapen upper lip. His eyes began to dart between them, wild with fear. "You're crazy, Hatcher. I didn't have nothing to do with Freddy Morris. Me? You kidding?"

"No. I'm not kidding. You want to change your mind about that lawyer?"

Gordie was too upset for that to register. "I . . . I never shot nobody. I'm scared of guns. They make me nervous."

"That's why we're not charging you with first degree. We don't believe you made poor Freddy lie down in that marsh, cut out his tongue, and then popped him in the back of the head with a forty-five." He pretended to fire a pistol and made a loud noise with his mouth.

Gordie flinched. "I gotta go to the bathroom."

"You can hold it."

"Duncan," DeeDee said.

"I *said*, he can hold it."

She looked at Gordie with sympathy and raised her shoulders in a helpless shrug.

"Look, Gordie," Duncan said, "we know, those narcs outside know, the Feds know, we all know you gave Freddy Morris over to Savich."

"Are you nuts? *Savich?* He scares me worse than guns. If Freddy had been smarter, he would have been scared of him, too, and kept his trap shut."

Duncan looked over at DeeDee with a complacent grin, as though expecting her to congratulate him for scoring a point. Too late, Gordie realized that he'd given himself away. Immediately he tried to rectify it. "At least that was the word on the street. I heard that Freddy Morris, uh, you know, was in conversation with y'all. I didn't have personal knowledge of it."

"I think you did, Gordie," Duncan countered smoothly.

"No," he said, shaking his head adamantly. "Not me. Un-unh."

He squirmed in his chair. He wiped his damp palms on the thighs of his grimy blue jeans. He blinked hard as though clearing his vision.

Duncan let him stew for a moment, then said, "Tell me about Savich."

"He's a tough customer. So I hear. I only know him by reputation."

"You work for him. You cook and sell meth for him."

"I peddle some dope now and then, yeah. I don't know where it comes from."

"It comes from Savich."

"Naw, naw, he's a mechanic, ain't he? Makes machines or something?"

"You think I'm queer, Gordie?" Duncan asked angrily.

"Huh? No!"

"Is that what you think?"

"No, I—"

"Then stop jerking me around. You're not clever enough to outsmart me. You're one of Savich's most reliable mules. We've got schoolkids who testified at your last trial, Gordie, remember? They said under oath that they go to you for a sure score."

"I admitted to dealing every now and then. Didn't I?" He turned to DeeDee, frantically seeking her backing. "Didn't you hear me just admit that?"

"You're far too humble, Gordie," Duncan said. "Savich depends on you to make addicts, future customers, out of children. You've introduced them to meth. You've got them raiding their folks' medicine cabinets for boxes of Sudafed. You're an asset to Savich's operation."

The little man swallowed hard. "Far as I know, his operation is that machine shop."

"Are you afraid that if you talk about him to us, you'll wind up like Freddy Morris did?"

"What I heard? I heard . . . I heard Freddy bought it over some woman. A guy, I don't know who, did Freddy on account of he was banging his old lady. That's the story I got."

Duncan spoke softly, but with menace. "You're jerking me around again."

"I ain't gonna say nothing about Savich," the convict cried out, his voice tearing. He tapped the tabletop with a dirty, chipped fingernail. "You'll never get me to say anything, neither. Not now, not ever."

He appealed to DeeDee, whining, "Where's the confession? Those first cops that arrested me? They said it would take a while to draw up the paperwork. Left me waiting here, and in come those narcs, harassing me. Now y'all. Just let me sign a confession saying I went at that guy last night with a broken beer bottle. Lock me up. I'm ready to take my punishment."

"We could make a deal—" DeeDee began.

"No deal," he said with a stubborn shake of his head.

"We could make this assault with a deadly weapon charge disappear like that." Duncan snapped his fingers an inch away from Gordie's flat nose. "Or we could lay several others on you. We might even ratchet this charge up to attempted murder. You'd do more time."

"Fine. You do that, Hatcher," he said, calling Duncan's bluff. "I'd rather go to jail than . . . Nothing," he finished in a mumble.

"Than wind up like Freddy Morris?" DeeDee asked.

But even her seeming gentleness didn't make a dent. She and Duncan continued with him for another half hour. He would not incriminate Savich. "Not even for spittin' on the sidewalk," he avowed.

They left him alone, not showing their weariness until they were out of the room. DeeDee slumped against the wall. "I've never had to try so hard to be nice. I wanted to wring it out of the little jerk."

"You were convincing. Even I thought you were turning soft." Duncan was teasing, and she knew it, but neither was in the mood for levity.

"Y'all did the best you could," said one of the narcotics officers gazing morosely at the video monitor, where Gordie could be seen gnawing at a bleeding cuticle. "Can't say as I blame him. Freddy Morris had his tongue cut out. Savich got to Chet Rollins in prison.

Somebody crammed a bar of soap down his gullet. He died slow. And that Andre . . . what was his last name?"

"Bonnet," Duncan supplied.

"No sooner had the DEA struck a deal with him to testify against Savich than his house blows up, his mother, his girlfriend, and her two kids in there with him."

"Savich got a hung jury and that screwup ADA ruined us for a retrial," Duncan said. "He got away with killing five people. The baby was three months old."

"We thought we had Morris locked down tight," the narc said, taking out his frustration on his chewing gum. "That Savich is one smart sumbitch."

"He's not that smart," Duncan growled. "We'll get him."

"Doesn't look like we're going to get him with Gordie Ballew's help," the second narc said.

"Even if he made a deal with us, Gordie isn't a good candidate." They all looked to Duncan to elaborate on his statement. "First off, he's scared shitless of Savich. He'd give himself away before you could set up the sting. Secondly, he's resigned to spending most of his life behind bars.

"In fact, I think he wants to. Why would he risk dying violently by ratting out Savich, when he can be guaranteed three squares a day and a home where everybody else is just as bad off as he is? For someone as pathetic as Gordie, that's about the best deal available."

They all muttered agreement of sorts. Duncan and DeeDee left the others to wrap up getting Gordon Ballew's confession to the assault charge.

"Who do we know I could get to sweep my house for electronic bugs?"

By tacit agreement, Duncan and DeeDee had regrouped in his office. She was opening a can of Diet Coke when he asked his surprise question, nearly causing her to spill the drink.

"You think your house is *bugged?*"

He told her about his overnight guest.

She listened, her mouth slack with disbelief. "Duncan, you stupid—"

"I know, I know." He raised his hands in surrender. "I was an idiot. I confess. But it happened. Now I've got to do some damage control."

"She could have killed you."

"Savich is saving that particular honor for himself. This was just another taunt, his way of letting me know how vulnerable I am."

"Was she worth it?"

"I don't even remember," he admitted. "I didn't know anything until you called and woke me up. When she dropped that bombshell, I bounded out of bed and chased her downstairs. She struck off down the sidewalk at a run. I would've gone after her, but realized I was bare-assed, unarmed, and that possibly that was the plan. Savich could be waiting out there in the bushes, ready to pop me the minute I appeared. So I went back in, got my weapon, and searched the house, thinking he might be inside. He wasn't, of course. Far as I can tell, nothing was disturbed."

"Except her side of the bed."

"You couldn't resist, could you?"

"Did she take anything?"

"I don't think so. I didn't notice anything missing. But while I was asleep she might have planted some kind of surveillance equipment in my house. I want it checked as soon as possible."

Within half an hour, they'd run down a surveillance expert who sometimes did contract work for the department. He promised to do the sweep later that morning. Duncan gave him the location of his hidden key as well as the code of his alarm system, which he'd changed before leaving the house.

As he concluded the call, DeeDee stacked her hands atop the mass of steel wool that passed for hair, and sighed with resignation. "What am I going to do with you?"

"Send me to my room?"

"Did you at least use a condom?"

"I did."

"Well, that's something. And you're being conscientious about setting your house alarm. That's good. But from now on, get references before you take a woman to bed, okay? If Savich is—"

"Cato Laird lied to us."

She dropped her hands from her head. "I thought we were discussing Savich."

"Now we're discussing the Lairds."

"You learned something yesterday after sending me away from the country club, didn't you? You fibbed when you told me nothing came out of your locker room chat with the judge. Waste of time, you said."

He'd called her on his cell phone from the taxi he'd taken from the club to his town house. "Yeah, I fibbed."

"How come?"

"Because I wanted to take an evening off."

"Look how that turned out," she said drolly.

"I knew if I even hinted that I'd learned something potentially important, neither of us would have had a night off, and in my estimation, both of us needed one."

"I could kill you," she snarled. "But not before you tell me what you found out."

"He lied to us about Meyer Napoli."

He recounted everything Judge Laird had told him about hiring the private investigator to follow Elise. "He's so crazy in love, he doesn't care that their marriage has cost him the respect of friends and associates. Possibly even his next reelection. They share a passionate sexual appetite for each other. Even though she had an affair, he loved her too much to confront her with it. It's over. History. The marriage remains intact. Everyone's happy."

"She doesn't know that he hired Napoli?"

"He says she doesn't."

"So the lady was telling the truth when she claimed she'd never heard of him."

"I guess."

"And the judge is convinced the affair is over?"

"Oh, it's over, all right."

DeeDee looked at him quizzically.

"Mrs. Laird's lover was Coleman Greer."

CHAPTER
12

T HEY WENT TO BREAKFAST IN A DOWNTOWN COFFEE SHOP NEAR the Barracks. DeeDee ordered an egg white omelet with fat-free cheese, fresh tomatoes, and whole wheat toast. Duncan had two eggs over easy, fluffy grits with melting butter, sausage links, and biscuits with gravy.

"That's so unfair," DeeDee remarked as she watched him dunk a piece of sausage into the gravy. "I'm having a voodoo doll made of you. Every time I have to eat low-cal, I'm going to poke a needle into it."

"It'll catch up with me one of these days."

"I doubt it," she muttered. "It's genetic. One of God's meanest jokes on the human race is that you get to see what you're going to become. Have you seen my mother's butt? Broad as a barn."

"But she's not wrinkled."

"Because her face is as round as a pie plate. I'm seeing them today." Visits with her parents always put her in a bad and self-critical mood.

"You'll eat well there."

"But not until we've gone to the cemetery and paid homage to precious Steven." Then she placed her palm against her forehead and rubbed it hard. "Listen to me. My brother is dead, I'm alive, and I'm resenting *him?* What kind of person does that make me? A terrible person, that's what."

"Look, if you'd rather have this conversation with yourself alone, I can leave and come back later."

She shot Duncan a wry smile. "Sorry. But you know how I hate those pilgrimages to Steven's grave. Mom sobs. Dad turns as silent as the headstone. As we leave, he looks at me and I know what he's thinking. He's thinking why, if he had to lose one of his children, it had to be Steven."

"That's not what he's thinking."

"Oh, yeah? Then why does he make me feel like I'm a colossal disappointment?"

"He just doesn't know how to show you how proud he is. He loves you." This is what Duncan always told her, but he knew she didn't believe it. He wasn't sure he believed it himself.

DeeDee's brother had been killed in a car accident a week before his high school graduation. DeeDee, several years younger, had taken it upon herself to fill her brother's shoes, or try. Two decades after the tragedy, her parents were still mourning him and she was still trying to make up for their loss and win the love they had lavished on her dead sibling, their fair-haired child.

Her father had been a career military man. So straight out of college DeeDee had joined the Marines. She'd had a perfect service record, but it had failed to impress her father. She declined to reenlist when her stint was up and signed on with the SPD instead. Working her way up through the ranks, she'd made detective in record time, asked for VCU, and got it.

She had a natural aptitude for police work, and seemed to thrive on it. But Duncan often wondered if her career choice was yet another attempt to prove to her parents that she could do a difficult job as well as, or better than, any man. As well as, or better than, Steven could have.

Her goal-setting and overachieving were admirable. But the quest for excellence that made her a good cop also made her a discontented individual. Never satisfied with her performance, she was constantly striving to do better. She worked to the exclusion of everything else. She had few friends and took even fewer occasions to socialize. She scorned the very idea of a romantic relationship, saying that it wouldn't be worth the effort required to make it work, and if by some miracle it did work, it wouldn't coalesce with her career.

Many times Duncan had pointed out how lopsided her life was and urged her to give it some balance. But obsession was a tough adversary to argue against. Once a person became that grafted to something, it ruled her life, governed her decisions, and ultimately could lead to calamity.

His mind stumbled and fell over that last thought.

Whose obsession had he been thinking about? DeeDee's or his own? He'd been dangerously close to obsessing over Savich. Now, Elise Laird.

"Duncan?"

DeeDee jarred him out of the disturbing introspection. "Huh?"

"I said let's talk about Elise Laird's affair with Coleman Greer."

Swell.

"That hunka hunka burning love," she said, in tune to the Elvis song.

"I didn't know you were such a fan."

"Duh."

"Good ballplayer."

"Good? All-Star, Duncan. For the three seasons he was with the Braves."

"I know the statistics. Better than you, I bet," he added, wondering why he was suddenly feeling so cross with the world, and with DeeDee in particular. Could it be because she thought Coleman Greer was a hunka hunka burning love, and, apparently, so had Elise?

"What are your thoughts on their affair?" DeeDee asked.

Stalling, he signaled the waitress to refill his coffee cup. The question went unanswered until their plates had been cleared away and he was sipping the fresh brew.

"It hasn't been confirmed that they had an affair." Even as he said that, he knew DeeDee's reaction would probably be volatile. It was.

"Oh, please! Give me a break. A woman has secret meetings with Coleman Greer, and you don't think they were doing the nasty thing? What else would they have been doing?"

He couldn't think of a plausible alternative to the nasty thing.

She said, "Let me tell you what I think."

"I never doubted that you would."

"I think the chances are very good that Mrs. Laird lied when she said she'd never heard of Meyer Napoli. No, let me finish," she said when she saw that he was about to interrupt. "She copped that innocent act for our sake as well as for her husband's. I think she somehow discovered that Napoli was following her. She figured it had to have been her husband who hired him to do so. And she confronted Napoli."

"You're outdoing yourself, DeeDee. Jumping to conclusions without having anything to back them up. Zilch. Zero."

"Hear me out."

He shrugged and indicated for her to continue.

"She confronts Napoli, who, we know, has the morals of a maggot. She pays him more than her husband does. He returns to Cato empty-handed. . . . What?" she asked when Duncan began shaking his head.

"Laird told me that Napoli brought him evidence of the affair, but he refused to hear it or see it, remember?"

She gnawed on that for a moment, then said, "Okay, then maybe Napoli went to her. Later. After the judge had dismissed him. He shows her pictures, video, some kind of proof of her cheating. Tells her that maybe her husband is no longer interested in the material, but others would be. Media, perhaps. Coleman Greer is news, et cetera. He blackmails her. It's not beyond Napoli to double-dip like that."

"No, but where does Gary Ray Trotter factor in?"

"Messenger boy."

"She shot the messenger?"

"Something like that."

Duncan was reluctant to admit that all day yesterday, after his conversation with the judge, his thoughts had clicked along the same track. Cato Laird had lied about knowing Meyer Napoli outside the courtroom. Elise could have lied just as easily, and perhaps more convincingly.

"Your scenario isn't without merit," he said. "But as long as we're being creative and playing make-believe—"

DeeDee made a face at him.

"—let's look at it from another perspective. Let's say that Napoli had been blackmailing the judge. He's got the goods on the judge's wife and her famous baseball-player lover. The judge may not want to know the lurid details, but you can bet the public does."

"To avoid exposure, the judge pays Napoli to keep his wife's affair a family secret," DeeDee said.

"Exactly. His Honor is playing both ends against the middle. He doesn't want the dirt on his wife to become public, and he doesn't want his wife to know he's got the dirt." He closed his eyes to better concentrate.

"What?" DeeDee said after a time.

The scenario he'd constructed moved him only a hair's breadth away from believing Elise's allegation. But he had to be very careful how he presented it to DeeDee. "What if . . ."

"What?" she pressed.

"What if Judge Laird isn't quite as forgiving and forgetful of the affair as he wanted me to believe? What if it's been eating at him? A cancer on the marriage, on his love for his wife, on his ego and manhood?"

DeeDee frowned. "He'd have to be one damn fine actor. He seems to worship the ground on which she treads."

"I'm only playing 'what if?' " he said irritably.

"Okay. Go on."

"The night of the shooting, he kept her in bed, didn't let her set the alarm."

"We don't know that he *kept* her in bed."

He did. At least that's what Elise had told him. "Let's assume."

"Wait," DeeDee said, holding up her hand like a traffic cop. "Are you saying . . . ? What are you saying? Where are you going with this? That Trotter wasn't simply Napoli's go-between? That he was there for a more nefarious purpose?"

Duncan shrugged as though to say it was possible, wasn't it? "He had a pistol, which he fired."

"Gary Ray Trotter? An enforcer? Some kind of hired gunman sent to put pressure on Judge Laird?"

"Or Mrs. Laird."

"I hate to speak disrespectfully of the dead, but, Duncan, come on. Gary Ray Trotter, hired assassin?"

"You don't think that idea has legs?"

"Not even stumps."

Actually, neither did he. The more he thought about it, the less likely it seemed that a man of Cato Laird's intelligence and resources would hire a chronic screwup like Trotter to do his killing for him. Elise Laird was playing him for a chump. He just didn't know why. And he was furious with himself for giving her any credence at all.

But why would she make up a story like that? *To protect herself from prosecution, stupid.*

Why would she come to him with it? Even stupider. He had lust in his heart and she knew it.

But, dammit, she'd seemed genuinely scared when he said he might simply ask Cato what motive he could have for wanting his wife dead. Was that motive her affair with Coleman Greer?

"Shit!"

"What?" DeeDee asked in response to his expletive.

"I don't know what. I've gone round and round on this thing and still all we've really got is a fatal shooting that doesn't add up. It's . . ."

"Hinky."

"For lack of a better word. But the deeper we go, the less—"

"It looks like self-defense."

"But nothing we have contradicts self-defense."

"Then why are we spending so much time on it?"

"I don't know."

"Yeah, you do."

Yeah, he did, but he wasn't yet willing to tell DeeDee about Elise Laird's note, her visit to his town house, and her allegation that her husband had hired Gary Ray Trotter to kill her.

"We're not closing the book on it because of our intuition. We both feel we're missing something," she said. "And that something could mean the difference between A: a woman protecting herself from a home intruder."

"Or B: a homicide."

"A significant difference." She watched the waitress serve another diner a slice of coconut cream pie. "If Elise Laird eats like that, I'll kill myself."

"You don't like her, do you?"

"I hate her," she said bluntly. "Isn't it enough that she looks like Helen of Troy and lives a life of luxury in a frigging mansion? It's just too much to take that she also got to see Coleman Greer naked."

"That's not hate, that's jealousy."

"Before, it was jealousy," she said. "It's graduated to hate now that I know about her and Coleman Greer."

"We need to confront her about that." Duncan swore to himself that his interest in Elise's affair with the baseball player was strictly business. It could be integral to their investigation. He needed to see her reaction when Greer's name was mentioned. But *only* because her reaction could be telling and therefore important to the case. Honest.

"I couldn't agree more," DeeDee said. "We need to ask her about it, let her know that we know." Her eyes narrowed the way they did when she was at the shooting range, taking aim at a target. "I particularly want to know if she was responsible for his suicide."

CHAPTER

13

Shortly after noon on Monday, DeeDee bounded into Duncan's office. "I just got off the phone with her. She'll be here in five minutes."

"That soon?"

"That soon. I got her on her cell. She was out running errands, said she'd come straight here."

After breakfast, they had decided to give themselves, as well as Elise Laird, a free Sunday. DeeDee had gone to her parents' home for dinner. She called it "paying penance."

He'd gone to his gym in the afternoon and worked out, including fifty laps in the pool. He spent the remainder of the day at home, which the electronic surveillance guy had told him was bug-free. He was only mildly relieved to hear it.

Savich hadn't sent the woman to plant any bugs, but to send a message: Savich could get to him whenever he was good and ready, and, as Duncan had feared, he probably wouldn't see it coming.

He'd watched TV, worked a crossword puzzle, played the piano. These pastimes didn't require one to be armed with a lethal weapon. Nevertheless, he'd kept his pistol with him. He'd slept with it.

He'd thought about Elise. More than was good for him.

When he and DeeDee arrived at the office this morning, they'd discussed how they were going to handle the upcoming interview with Elise. It would be tricky to question her about her affair with Coleman Greer without revealing that they'd learned of it through her husband. Duncan didn't want to incur the judge's wrath if he could avoid it.

"Did she ask what we want to talk to her about?" he asked DeeDee now.

"I told her it was a delicate subject and that we wanted to protect her privacy as much as possible."

"Huh. She didn't pursue it?"

"Nope."

"She say anything about the judge?"

"Only that she intended to ask him to join us."

"Shit."

"But I dissuaded her, again hinting that she would want to keep this confidential."

"He'll have our hides if he finds out about it."

DeeDee said, "I'm banking she won't be the one to tell him. If Judge Laird is right, she never knew that he had knowledge of her affair. Why would she confess it to him now?"

"It may be the lesser of two evils. She may own up to the affair if she's faced with an indictment."

"Admit to committing adultery, but deny murdering Trotter."

"Not a tough choice," he said. "Especially if your husband has already forgiven you."

"Hubby also knows the ins and outs of murder trials," DeeDee said. "He knows the best defense attorneys, and price wouldn't be an issue. The judge could save her skinny tush."

But would he? Duncan wondered. Not if Elise's claim that he wanted to kill her was true.

"We could clear up a lot of this if we could talk to Napoli," DeeDee remarked, breaking into his thoughts.

"Kong says he's got no leads. They can't even locate his car. No airline ticket or bus ticket."

"Boat rental?"

Duncan shook his head as his desk phone buzzed.

"Maybe Napoli was raptured, taken straight to heaven."

"That was going to be my next guess." He answered the phone

and was informed that Mrs. Laird had arrived and was in the lobby. He covered the mouthpiece. "Where should we do this? Interrogation room?"

"Let's keep it as friendly as possible," DeeDee suggested. "How about right here?"

He told the receptionist that Detective Bowen would come down and escort Mrs. Laird to the VCU. While DeeDee was gone, he wedged another chair into his cramped office, then caught himself checking his shirttail and straightening his necktie. What the hell? he thought querulously. He didn't have a date with her; this was an interrogation.

DeeDee was chattering like a magpie, making friendly small talk as she led Elise down the space that separated the detectives' desks. Elise, on the other hand, didn't say anything until she reached the open door of his office. "Hello, Detective Hatcher."

"Thank you for coming on such short notice."

He offered her a chair. DeeDee took the other. He sat down at his desk. "We—"

"Should I call a lawyer?"

"If you like," he replied.

She glanced at DeeDee, then back at him. "Before you ask me a question, I have one for you."

"Fair enough."

"Why are you investigating the shooting at my home as though it's a homicide?"

"We're not," DeeDee said.

But Elise's gaze didn't waver from his. "What do you know, or think you know, that prevents you from accepting that I shot that man in self-defense?"

"If you polled the murderers in prison, Mrs. Laird, probably ninety-nine percent of them would claim they killed in self-defense. We can't simply take their word for it."

"Nor mine, it seems."

The softened pitch of her voice hinted that she was referring to more than just the question of self-defense. He hadn't taken her word about Cato Laird wanting her dead, either. "Nor yours," he said.

She took a steadying breath. "Why did you ask me to come here today?"

"What about the attorney?" DeeDee asked.

"First, tell me what this is about."

"Coleman Greer."

Caught completely off-guard, she breathed out in a gust. *"What?"*

"You knew the late Coleman Greer, All-Star first baseman for the Atlanta Braves."

She darted a look toward Duncan, then addressed her nod to DeeDee. "I knew him well. We were friends."

"Friends?"

"Yes."

No one said anything for several moments. Duncan and DeeDee waited to see if she would elaborate, but she appeared shell-shocked. Finally she looked at Duncan. "What about Coleman?"

Before he could answer, DeeDee said, "He was an amazing athlete."

"He was very talented."

"Were you a fan?"

"More his friend than a fan. I don't follow the sport that closely."

"How did you two meet?"

"We grew up together." Seeing their surprise, she continued. "Junior high. High school. We were from the same small town in central Georgia."

"Were you high school sweethearts?"

"No, Detective Bowen. Friends."

"Did you maintain this friendship after high school?"

"That was difficult. Coleman got a baseball scholarship. After college he was drafted into the minors. I'm sure you know all this," she said to Duncan.

"I know about his baseball career. I don't know about his personal relationships. That's what we want to know. About your relationship with him."

"Why? What relevance does it have?"

"That's what we're trying to determine."

"There's nothing to *determine*," she said. "How did you even know that Coleman and I were friends?"

"We have our ways."

It was such an inane statement that Duncan echoed the look of derision that Elise shot DeeDee. He said, "You lost contact with him while he was in college and the minor leagues?"

"Playing baseball consumed all his time. We sent birthday cards, Christmas greetings. But beyond that, we didn't stay in close contact."

"When was the last time you saw him?"

She looked away, said quietly, "A few days before he died."

"Before he killed himself," DeeDee said bluntly.

Head lowered, Elise nodded.

"Did he give you any indication that he planned to end his life?"

She raised her head and glared at DeeDee. "If he had, don't you think I'd have done something to stop him?"

"I don't know. Would you?"

DeeDee's harsh question left her dumbfounded. She stared at DeeDee for several beats, then turned to Duncan. "I don't understand this. Why are you asking me questions about Coleman?"

"They're painful for you?"

"Of course."

"Why?"

"He was my friend!"

"And lover."

"What?"

"I need to repeat it?"

"No, but you're wrong. We weren't lovers. We were friends." DeeDee made a snorting sound of disbelief, but Elise ignored it. Her attention was focused on Duncan. "I thought this was about Gary Ray Trotter. What does Coleman have to do with that? With anything?"

"When did you reestablish contact with him? More contact than birthday cards and such."

"He called and invited me to come see him in Atlanta."

"Was your husband included in this reunion?"

"No, this was right when Coleman started playing for the

Braves. I hadn't even met Cato. Later, after I was married, I invited Coleman to our home for dinner. Cato is a Braves fan, so he was delighted to learn that Coleman and I were friends."

"They liked each other?"

"Very well."

"Except for that one dinner, did they ever socialize?"

"Coleman arranged for us to sit in a box at one of the home games. We met him afterward for dinner. As far as I know, those are the only two occasions he and Cato were together."

Duncan got up from his chair and sat on the corner of his desk, so he'd have the advantage of height and would be looking down at her. "You know very well that they never saw each other again, because it would've been messy to have your husband and your lover—"

"Coleman was not my lover."

"You never saw him alone, without your husband?"

She faltered. "I didn't say that."

"So you did see him alone."

"Sometimes."

"Often?"

"Coleman's schedule was—"

"Often?"

Relenting to his pressure, she nodded. "Whenever our schedules allowed it."

"Where did you meet?"

"Usually here in Savannah."

"Where, here in Savannah?"

"Different places."

"Restaurants? Bars?"

"Coleman tried to avoid public places. Fans wouldn't leave him alone."

"So you met in places that afforded you privacy?"

"Yes."

"Like hotel rooms?"

She hesitated, then nodded.

"What did your husband think of these rendezvous in hotel rooms?"

She didn't respond.

"He didn't know about them, did he?" Duncan continued. "You didn't inform him when you were going to meet a popular, good-looking superstar like Coleman Greer in a hotel room, did you? Because he wouldn't have liked it one bit."

She shot up from her chair. "I don't have to listen to this."

Duncan placed a hand on her shoulder. "You can listen to it here and now, alone, or you can listen to it later with a lawyer and your husband present."

He could feel her body heat radiating into his hand. Her breathing was rapid and light, agitated. "Coleman and I were friends. Only friends."

"Who had secret meetings in hotel rooms."

"Why don't you believe me?"

"Because nothing you've told me is credible." His eyes speared into hers. *"Nothing."*

"I've told you the truth."

"About you and Coleman Greer?"

"About everything."

"How long did these cozy get-togethers last? One hour? Two? Longer?"

"It varied."

"Ballpark. No pun intended."

"An hour or two. Usually no longer."

"Depending on how long you could sneak away."

She released a slow breath. "You're correct about that. Cato didn't know about these visits with Coleman."

"Ah."

"But it wasn't what you're thinking. It wasn't an affair."

"Hotel rooms are used for two things. One of them is sleeping. I don't think you met with Coleman Greer to sleep."

"We talked."

"Talked."

"Yes."

"That's it?"

"Yes."

"With all your clothes on?"

"Yes!"

"Do you honestly expect me to believe—"

"It's the truth!"

"—that you were in a hotel room with a man—"

"A *friend*."

"—and didn't get fucked?"

She inhaled a quick breath. She seemed about to speak, then thought better of it. Her lips compressed.

Duncan smirked. "That's what I thought."

Until she shrugged off his hand, he didn't realize that it had been clamping her shoulder all this time. "Are you arresting me, Detective Hatcher?"

"Not yet."

She retrieved her handbag and stormed out.

Her sudden departure left a vacuum in the small room. Duncan, staring at the empty doorway through which she had passed, raked his fingers through his hair and mumbled a stream of swear words. Long moments later, he realized DeeDee was still there, watching him, parallel frown lines between her eyebrows.

He raised his shoulders. "What?"

"What was that all about?"

"What?"

"The . . ." She sawed her hand back and forth, as though forming a connection between her chest and an invisible point in space. "That thing between the two of you."

"What thing?"

"Tension. Something. I don't know. Whatever it was, it was crackling."

"You're imagining things. Talking about Coleman Greer naked got your sap running."

"If you let this woman cloud your judgment, you're the sap."

He pounced on that. "Tell me how I exercised poor judgment."

"By letting her sail out of here."

"We don't have anything to justify holding her, DeeDee," he said, rather too loudly. "Without any evidence, how could I? I wanted to detain her, God knows."

Before walking out, she fired a parting shot. *"Detain?* Is that a new word for it?"

For the remainder of the afternoon, DeeDee stayed at her desk, cleaning up paperwork on another case. Duncan stayed at his desk, too, thinking about Elise and wondering if she was an accomplished liar or telling the truth, but ostensibly running his trotlines on Savich.

Going through the motions, he placed a call to his contact at the DEA. "He's been quiet," Duncan said. "Makes me nervous."

He learned from the agent that after getting a tip from an informant, they'd raided one of Savich's trucks. All they'd found was machinery and the proper shipping invoices that matched the cargo, right down to the correct serial numbers.

Duncan wasn't surprised. Savich wouldn't use his company trucks to ship drugs along Interstate 95. While the truck was being stripped down and searched, family vans and nondescript sedans loaded to the gills were headed for the lucrative markets along the eastern seaboard.

He consoled the agent over the failed mission. "I couldn't get him for Freddy Morris, either."

"You still dry?"

"As a bone," Duncan admitted. "Lucille Jones has gone underground, and the DA won't try the case again without something substantial, like the knife Savich used to cut out Freddy's tongue. He'd prefer it to still be dripping blood."

"Not gonna happen."

"One can dream."

Duncan's frustration matched that of the federal agent. He suspected that Savich was having information fed to him, probably by one of the department's own paid informants. Although, maybe not. Savich had infallible sensors that had served him well over the course of his criminal career. He may only have sensed Freddy Morris's betrayal and, taking no chances, acted with dispatch to eliminate him.

Ready to put an end to the unproductive Monday, Duncan left

for home early. On his way out, he stopped at DeeDee's desk. "What's your gut feeling?"

She didn't look up. "On?"

"Laird. Do we sign off on it? It was self-defense. Case closed."

"Is that what you want to do?"

"If we could talk to Napoli—"

"But we can't."

"And that's like an itch I can't scratch," he said. "The whole Napoli-Trotter-Laird connection."

"It would be useful to know what Napoli had on Mrs. Laird. How damaging was it?"

He stared out the window for a moment, then said decisively, "Let's keep working it. Give it a few more days. Maybe Napoli will surface."

She looked up at him then, her smile bright. "See you tomorrow."

However, less than an hour later, she called him on his cell phone. "What are you doing?"

"Buying groceries," he replied.

"Groceries? You don't cook."

"So far I've got toilet paper and beer."

"Essentials, for sure."

Relieved that they were friends again, he asked, "What's up?"

"We've been summoned to appear at the Lairds' house at eight o'clock."

"Tonight?"

"Yep."

"What for?"

"I don't think it's for dinner."

"Meet you there."

At thirty seconds to eight, they met on the walkway leading up to the front door of the stately residence. "Any ideas?" he asked.

"He just said to be here at eight, and here we be."

"Why'd he call you?"

"I was the one still in the office." DeeDee punched the doorbell and they heard the chime inside the house. "We probably shouldn't count on getting a full confession."

"To what?"

"To anything."

Mrs. Berry answered the door and regarded them as though they smelled like raw sewage. "They're waiting for you."

She led them as far as the arched opening into the living room. Cato Laird was standing with his back to the fireplace and the painting with the dead rabbit lying among the fresh vegetables. Elise was seated on the sofa. Both wore solemn expressions, but his voice was cordial enough when he thanked them for coming and asked them to take seats. There was no offer of refreshments on this visit.

The judge sat down beside his wife on the sofa. He took her hand and patted it reassuringly. "Elise told me about her interview with you earlier today. My initial reaction was to call Bill Gerard and raise hell. You placed my wife at a terrible disadvantage."

Prudently, Duncan and DeeDee remained silent.

"But on second thought, I changed my mind about filing a complaint. You deserve a dressing-down for pulling a stunt like that, but I didn't want to put any additional stress on Elise.

"And, actually, I was more angry with myself than with you. It's my fault that she had to undergo that unpleasant interrogation. I couldn't live with that." He glanced at her, then came back to them. "So I confessed to her that I'd hired Meyer Napoli to follow her."

Duncan's gaze moved to Elise. She was regarding him with palpable hostility.

The judge said, "I felt that Elise should know everything that was said during our conversation in the locker room the other day, Detective Hatcher. I'm not proud of myself for lying to you and Detective Bowen when I said I'd never had personal dealings with Napoli. I deeply regret my business with him, especially if it resulted in the shooting of Trotter, no matter how roundabout the connection was."

"That was our thinking when we talked to Mrs. Laird today," DeeDee said. "That Trotter's break-in was somehow related to Meyer Napoli."

"My business with him was so short-lived," the judge said, "I still hold firm to my theory that Trotter was acting alone, and that any connection he had to Napoli was coincidental. But looking at it from the perspective of an investigator, I'll admit it warranted closer examination, particularly if Napoli had proof of an affair between Coleman Greer and my wife.

"So," he went on, "I felt we should clear the air. Hopefully by explaining a couple of outstanding issues, we can put this regrettable incident behind us once and for all. Now that there are no lingering secrets between Elise and me, we can be perfectly frank with you. Fire away."

DeeDee plunged right in. "Mrs. Laird, *does* Napoli have proof of an affair between you and Coleman Greer?"

"No such proof exists, Detective Bowen. There was no affair."

Reading the skepticism in DeeDee's face, the judge said, "You will believe her after she explains the nature of their relationship."

"She told us they were friends," DeeDee said.

"I told you we were *close* friends. To have something ugly made of our friendship offends me deeply." As she said this, she shot Duncan a drop-dead look. "It pains me to have to talk about him at all, but since you give me no choice . . ." She paused and took a deep breath. "He and I dated a few times in high school, but it was always platonic, never sexual, not even romantic. We were pals, confidantes."

DeeDee asked, "If you were so close, why didn't you know he was contemplating suicide?"

"I knew that Coleman was depressed, but I didn't realize the depth of his depression. I wish I had."

"He was at the top of his game," Duncan said. "What did he have to be depressed about?"

"His heart was broken."

The simple statement took him and DeeDee aback. He said, "That begs for an explanation, Mrs. Laird."

"Coleman's lover was leaving him."

"But you weren't that lover."

"No," she said firmly. "I was not."

"So all those times that you met him secretly, you—"

"I provided him a shoulder to cry on."

"You didn't have a carnal relationship."

"How many times must I repeat it, Detective Hatcher?"

The judge said, "They still don't believe you, darling. They won't believe you until you tell them what you told me."

She gave Duncan a long, measured look, as though willing him to accept what she was about to say. "Coleman didn't have a sexual relationship with me or any woman. His lover was Tony Esteban. His teammate."

CHAPTER
14

EVEN SO FAR INLAND, ATLANTA WAS AS SULTRY AS SAVANNAH. The heat sucked the breath out of Duncan as he exited the airport to hail a cab. The driver was friendly and talkative, keeping up a lively chatter as he negotiated the expressway traffic toward Buckhead, where Tony Esteban owned the penthouse of a high-rise condo.

Duncan had woken up early, knowing he was going to come to Atlanta. He didn't tell anybody, not even DeeDee, who would have wanted to come with him. He figured the Braves' Puerto Rican treasure would be reluctant to discuss his sex life with cops, but that one would be less intimidating than two.

Besides, he was grateful to have a break from DeeDee. After leaving the judge and his wife last night, they'd driven separately to a restaurant, where Duncan ate a late supper, and DeeDee imbibed Diet Coke by the quart and railed endlessly against Elise Laird and her lies.

"I can't believe she had the nerve to say that Coleman Greer was gay! That's what she wants us to believe? As if!"

"It goes against stereotype, but that doesn't mean—"

"Coleman Greer was *not* gay."

She wouldn't listen to any argument to the contrary and rebuked both Duncan and the judge for giving any credence to it whatsoever.

"She's got her husband by the dick. He'll believe it because he wants to. She's so damn clever. She told him the one lie where he could save face. She let herself off the hook *and* salvaged his wounded pride. That takes talent. She's a player, Duncan. The likes of which I've never seen."

When he could work in a word edgewise, he'd said, "Even if what she claims about Greer is false, that only makes her guilty of adultery. We're no closer to having evidence that she plugged Gary Ray Trotter for any reason other than self-defense."

"It's still murky, Duncan."

Yes, it was. Murky enough for him to make the short flight from Savannah to Atlanta, paying his own way. He would try to get reimbursed later. Even if he wound up financing the trip himself, it would be worth the price of the airfare to get to the truth. Was Elise Laird a manipulative liar? If so, the investigation into the fatal shooting would continue. If not, her own life was at risk.

Either way, he had to know.

The driver pulled the taxi into the porte cochere of the high-rise and remarked on its swankiness. Duncan agreed. He paid the man and walked into the marble lobby, which embraced him with refrigerated air, the scent of lilies, and soft music. The reception desk was manned by a uniformed concierge.

"Good morning, sir. Can I help you?"

"Morning. I'm here to see Mr. Anthony Esteban." He reached for his ID wallet, and in doing so made certain the man could see the holster beneath his sport jacket.

The concierge cleared his throat. "Is Mr. Esteban expecting you?"

Duncan flashed him a wide smile. "I didn't want to spoil the surprise."

"I'll have to buzz him."

"Whatever. No rush."

Belying his nonchalance, he leaned forward over the tall desk and watched with interest as the concierge raised a telephone receiver to his ear, then pressed the call button for the penthouse. "Mr. Esteban, I hate to disturb you. There's a gentleman here, asking to see you. A Mr. . . . uh . . ."

"Detective Sergeant Duncan Hatcher, Savannah–Chatham Metropolitan Police Department." The city and county departments had officially merged a year ago. Duncan rarely used the full name. For one thing, it sounded stupid. For another, it was too long. In the time it took you to identify yourself to a felon, you could get killed. He really only used it when he wanted to look like a big shot.

The concierge repeated what he'd said, listened, then asked the baseball player to hold on. "He wants to know in regards to what."

"Elise Laird and an incident at her house last week."

Again, he repeated Duncan's words into the telephone receiver. After a brief pause, he said, "Mr. Esteban says he doesn't know an Elise Laird."

"Coleman Greer's friend."

The concierge's mouth formed a small, round O, then he passed along the message to Esteban. "Of course, Mr. Esteban." He hung up. "Go right up. The elevator bank is behind this wall."

"Thanks."

The elevator was so fast, Duncan's ears popped on the express ascent. The doors opened into a sizable foyer. Tony Esteban was waiting for him outside his front door. He was several inches shorter than Duncan, solidly built, and, Duncan knew, had arms that could knock the stitches out of a baseball. He was wearing nothing except a pair of workout shorts and a chunk of gold suspended from a half-inch-wide chain around his neck.

"Hatcher?"

"It's a pleasure, Mr. Esteban."

"Call me Tony," he said, extending his hand. "Come in." He spoke with only a trace of a Spanish accent.

"The proverbial glass house," Duncan remarked as he stepped into the penthouse and took a look around. Floor-to-ceiling windows afforded almost a 360-degree view of the city.

"You like it? Cost a fucking fortune."

"You make a fucking fortune."

He grinned the grin that had made him vastly popular with fans and the media. "You want something to drink?" He led Duncan across what seemed to be an acre of sparsely furnished living space to a wet bar. He pushed a concealed button that opened the mirrored doors behind the bar to reveal its stock. "Whatever you like. Scotch, bourbon, a milk shake? I got everything."

"How about a glass of ice water?"

He looked disappointed, but said okay. Duncan expected him to step behind the bar, so he was surprised when he hollered, "Jenny!"

Within seconds Jenny appeared. All six feet of her, most of it sleek, tanned legs that looked like they'd been airbrushed to perfection. Her hair was the color of a sunset, her breasts were huge, and she was gorgeous. She was wearing a miniskirt, high-heeled sandals, and a tank top no bigger than a slingshot, which left absolutely nothing to the imagination. "Jenny, this is Mr. Hatcher."

"Hi, Mr. Hatcher."

Duncan found his voice. "How do you do, Jenny."

"Fine. Are you in baseball?"

"Uh, no."

"He's a cop from Savannah and he's thirsty. Fix him some ice water. Do me one of those protein shakes."

"Berries and yogurt?"

"Yeah, all that health stuff."

She went behind the bar to do his bidding. Esteban motioned Duncan toward one of the low white leather sofas in a grouping of similar pieces. The end tables were hammered metal and glass.

Once they were seated, Esteban asked, "You a baseball fan?"

"Yes."

"Braves?"

"Of course."

"Good." He beamed. "You ever play?"

"Some. Mostly football."

"Pro?"

Duncan smiled and shook his head. "I maxed out in college."

They filled the time it took Jenny to prepare their drinks talking about sports and the Braves' season so far. "Show him your ring, honey," Esteban said to her after she'd served their drinks. She extended her left hand toward Duncan, who praised the diamond, since it seemed that was expected.

"Almost ten carats," Esteban told him, though he hadn't asked.

"Wow." He smiled up at Jenny. "Is it an engagement ring?"

"He proposed in a hot air balloon," she simpered.

"In Napa," Esteban added. "One of those wine country things."

"Sounds romantic."

"It was," said Jenny.

"Have you set a date for the wedding?"

"Thanksgiving weekend. It can't be during the season."

"Right."

"Wedding, wedding, wedding is all she talks about. Flowers. Dresses. Shrimp cocktails. All that shit. Go on now, honey."

"It was nice to meet you, Mr. Hatcher. Bye."

"Bye."

Esteban affectionately smacked her heart-shaped butt as she strutted away, her heels tapping on the marble floor. As she disappeared through a set of double doors, he said, "She's something, huh?"

"She's amazing."

"I'm crazy about her. Have you ever seen a body like that?"

"Not that I can recall."

"She had some added to the top. I paid. She wanted them bigger, and I thought, what the hell? The bigger the better, right?"

"That's always been my motto." His wryness escaped the other man, who was too egotistical to hear anything except the sound of his own voice.

"She's a sweet kid. Goes through money like it was water, but it keeps her happy. And she keeps me happy. I'm telling you—and this is no exaggeration." He leaned in closer. "She could suck your eyeballs out through your dick."

"Impressive."

"You don't know the half of it." He took a drink of his shake and glanced at his wristwatch. "I got practice in an hour. How can I help you?"

"I'm investigating a fatal shooting."

"Fatal means somebody died, right?"

"Right. It took place last Thursday evening at the home of Judge Cato Laird and his wife, Elise."

"Yeah, I remember Elise. Now that you reminded me who she is. She's dead?"

"No." Duncan filled him in on the facts. He tried to avoid using words with more than five letters. "It seems Elise fired the fatal shot in self-defense. I'm just clearing up a few points."

"Like what?"

"I understand she had a close personal relationship with Coleman Greer."

He grimaced with obvious regret. "King Cole, we called him. What a fucking thing to do. You know, they think he'd been dead for a couple days before someone went to his place and checked on him. I heard it was a mess."

He'd blown the top of his head off. That could be messy, all right.

"What do you know about his relationship with Elise?"

"They went way back. Fuck buddies, you know? When there's nobody else around to fuck?"

"I'm familiar with the phrase."

"They were that kind of friends."

Duncan took a drink of his ice water and tried to look and sound casual. "When did you meet her?"

"He brought her to a Braves party, not long after he signed with the team. Knocked us all for a loop, 'cause she was such a babe and Cole had never said nothing about her. But he was low-key like that. Not a wild party guy."

"Are you a wild party guy?"

He laughed. "I do my share."

"Will marriage cramp your style?"

Esteban bobbed his eyebrows. "What happens on the road stays on the road. Know what I mean?"

"Gotcha."

Esteban held out his fist. Duncan bumped it with his, forming a male pact of silence. "So, King Cole brings Elise to a Braves party and she's a babe."

"Yeah."

"And?"

"And nothing." Esteban reached for his shake and took a slurp. "That's it."

"Really."

"Never saw her again and, as I said, Cole didn't talk about stuff like that. So, I guess that's all I can tell you."

Duncan leaned against the stiff leather back of the sofa and propped one ankle on the opposite knee. "Know what Elise told me? She told me that you and Coleman Greer were the fuck buddies, and that you were breaking it off, and that's why he put the barrels of that shotgun in his mouth and pulled the trigger."

Esteban's jaw went slack. He leaned forward, then back. He opened his mouth to speak but found he had no words. Finally he shook his head and said, "That bitch. That lying bitch!"

"It's not true?"

"Fucking A, it's not true." He bounded off his seat and began to prowl the marble floor, flinging deprecations in rapid-fire Spanish.

"Why would she say such a thing?" Duncan asked.

Esteban bore down on him. "Why? I'll tell you why. You want to know why?"

"Why?"

"Okay, it was like this. That night at the party?"

"The one where you said there was 'and nothing'?"

"I didn't want you to think I was a jerk, the kind of guy who would—"

"What happened at the party, Tony?"

"Cole got wasted. He passed out. That girl, that Elise, comes on to me. And I mean, man, she was hot for it. Hot, you know?"

"Okay."

"She's all over me. Made me nervous."

"Nervous?"

"Yeah, I didn't want my new teammate pissed at me over this chick, but she said it wasn't like that between her and Cole. Said they were friends and that he would want her to have a good time at the party. She was saying stuff like that all the time she's got her hand inside my pants. So I gave her what she wanted. Coupla times. I mean, she's great-looking. Why not, you know?"

Duncan made a guttural sound of acknowledgment.

Esteban sat back down. "She was good, man. I wouldn't have minded having some more of that, but the next morning, she's writing down all her phone numbers, asking when I'm gonna call, stuff like that.

"Every day after that, she's calling me, asking when she's going to see me, why haven't I called, didn't I like her, how dare I use her and then dump her like she was nothing."

He stopped suddenly. "You see that movie *Fatal Attraction*? That's what she was. That broad. That psycho bitch from hell. I expected to come home one day and find a fucking bunny boiling on my kitchen stove."

"Did you ever see her again?"

He shook his head. "I don't need that shit, man. I guess she gave up. She finally stopped calling."

"What did Coleman have to say about this?"

"He didn't know. At least, I didn't tell him. Don't know if she did." He frowned with disgust. "Man, I knew she was one twisted chick, and she swore she would pay me back for dumping her, but I didn't figure on her making up something like I'm gay. Gay? Jesus!" Then he chortled a laugh. "It's funny when you think about it."

"You took it upon yourself to go to Atlanta and see Tony Esteban?"

"Yes."

No sooner had Duncan cleared the door of the Barracks than he'd been summoned into Bill Gerard's office. Captain Gerard was a good cop with nearly forty years with the department. He was a fair supervisor who kept himself up to speed on all the cases the VCU was investigating, and he dispensed advice when asked for it. But he trusted the detectives under his supervision to do their jobs without having to be micromanaged.

However, when necessary, he could chew ass effectively. Duncan braced himself for a good one.

"The Braves management office called," Gerard said, stacking his freckled hands on his thinning ginger-colored hair. "They were steamed you didn't go through them to interview Esteban."

"I wanted to catch him unaware."

"Apparently you did, because after you left, he had second thoughts. He went whining to the team's PR people about a cop from Savannah asking him about a woman he barely knows who's involved in a fatal shooting. He was scared the media would get wind of it, blow it out of proportion, he'd wind up the cover story of *The National Enquirer.*

"The nervous PR people called Chief Taylor, who called me and wanted to know what the hell was going on." He spat into his dip cup and peered at Duncan over the top of his reading glasses. "I'd sorta like to know that myself, Dunk. What the hell's going on?"

"I'm not convinced the fatal shooting of Gary Ray Trotter was self-defense."

"Aw, shit."

Gerard liked to hunt and fish, read books about the Civil War, and make love to the wife he'd been married to since the night after his high school graduation. He was looking forward to enjoying those pastimes in retirement, which was only two years away. Until then, he wanted to do his job well, meeting its demands, but avoiding the snares of bureaucratic politics so that he could exit the police department gracefully and enemy-free.

"You think the judge's wife wasn't just protecting her life?"

"I think she may have been protecting her life*style.*"

"Shit," he repeated. "This isn't going to sit well with Cato Laird."

"I realize that, Bill. Believe me, I deliberated on it all the way back from Atlanta. He's chief judge of superior court. He presides over felony cases. The last thing a police department wants is a judge with a grudge against cops who bring those felons to court. This places the department in an awkward position. I understand and appreciate that. But it's my duty—"

Gerard held up his hand. "None of my detectives has to explain himself to me, Dunk. I trust you. Trust your instincts even more."

He wouldn't trust him so well if he knew the secrets Duncan had been keeping recently, the ethics he'd violated. Elise's note. His private encounter with her at his house. He wouldn't trust him so well if he knew how hard Duncan had struggled with his decision to pursue the case against her.

"What did Esteban say that implicated her?" Gerard asked.

"Is Kong here?"

Gerard looked at him with puzzlement. "I don't know, why?"

"I'd like for him and DeeDee to be in on this. That way I only have to tell it once."

"I'll go take a leak. You get them in here."

They reconvened five minutes later. DeeDee came in with a can of Diet Coke and an attitude. She was miffed at Duncan for going to Atlanta without her, or even telling her about the trip beforehand. He didn't let her pouting bother him. She'd get over it. Soon, unless he missed his bet. She'd suspected Elise of an ulterior motive all along, and he was about to provide one.

Kong was his hairy, sweaty, but affable self. "What up?" he asked Gerard.

The captain pointed to Duncan. "This is his meeting."

Duncan began by saying, "First of all, I'm giving notice here and now. When I grow up, I want to be a professional baseball player." His description of Tony Esteban's penthouse was designed to have them smiling, relaxed, and listening by the time he got down to the nitty-gritty.

"There was this red metal sculpture standing in the center of the room. It looked like an instrument of torture, or maybe a swan. And just like in the movies, he pushes a button, these smoky mirrored doors slide open, and there's a bar stocked with every conceivable potable."

They were raptly attentive by the time he got to Jenny. "Hugh Hefner never had it so good. Legs that went on forever. Tits out to here." He gestured with both hands, holding them away from his chest. "Right there on display beneath this tight tank top, and I'm talking—"

"We get it, Duncan," DeeDee said. "She had big tits. What did Esteban have to say?"

He gave the men a look that said there would be a more detailed description of Jenny's chest later, then recounted for them his conversation with Esteban.

When he finished, Gerard asked for clarification on a few points. "It was Mrs. Laird who told you Coleman Greer was gay?"

"Last night at their home," Duncan replied. "DeeDee and I were summoned there. Mrs. Laird was reluctant to destroy the myth—"

"It's no myth," DeeDee said.

"—of Coleman Greer's machismo, but she told us that after their high school romance, which was platonic—"

"Like hell," mumbled DeeDee.

"—he confessed to her what he'd never told another living soul. He was attracted to men."

" 'As God is my witness.' " DeeDee dramatically placed her hand over her heart. "Á la Scarlett O'Hara, she swore it."

"Jeez, I can't believe it," Kong said. "My boys would be crushed. I mean, not that there's anything wrong with it. Live and let live, I say. But . . . well, you'd rather your baseball heroes be straight." He looked around as though polling them. "Wouldn't you?"

"According to Esteban, Coleman Greer was straight."

"Correction, Bill," Duncan said. "According to Esteban, *he's* straight. He couldn't speak for Coleman Greer, and doesn't know with absolute certainty, but Esteban seriously doubts he was gay. How could he have been gay and nobody know? How could he have kept that hidden when he lived and traveled in the company of men half the year? He doesn't believe Coleman Greer was gay. But he *knows* that *he* 'ain't no fucking fag.' "

"Which blows a big hole in Elise Laird's story," DeeDee said. "I'm positive she invented that lie because it was the one her husband would grab on to with both hands. During all those trysts, she wasn't screwing her baseball player. No, she was consoling him over his gay love affair gone awry." She snuffled with scorn. "Priceless. Your affair is exposed by a PI your husband has hired to follow you. You need a lie, and quick. Voilà! Your lover isn't your lover. He doesn't even like girls."

"PI?" Kong said. "Here's where my missing person comes in, right? The PI was Napoli?"

Duncan said, "Anything?"

"Nothing. Not a hair off his greasy head."

"The judge hired *Napoli?*" Gerard said, his dismay showing.

"He said he was desperate to know if his wife was having an affair or if it was his imagination," Duncan explained. "He admitted to us that Napoli came through with something, but at the last minute he changed his mind, didn't want to learn what that something was."

"And Kong found Gary Ray Trotter's name among papers on Meyer Napoli's desk."

"That's right, Bill," Duncan said.

"Now I see where you're going with this," the captain said.

"Napoli had proof of Mrs. Laird's affair. The judge got cold feet, didn't want to know the truth after all, turned it down. But Napoli got greedy and took the proof to Mrs. Laird. He blackmailed her with it. Whether to protect herself, or Coleman Greer, or both of them, she agreed to a big payoff. Gary Ray Trotter was the drop man." He paused, then added, "This is all speculative, but it fits."

They sat in silence for a moment, pondering Duncan's summary. Kong was the first to speak. "But how'd she know Trotter would break in that particular night?"

"It could have been prearranged." Duncan told Gerard and Kong about her insomnia, her habit of going downstairs for milk. "Trotter may have been about to leave the goods, as instructed—"

"But she popped him first," DeeDee said. "Maybe he was firing his pistol in self-defense, not her."

"Maybe," Duncan said, tugging thoughtfully on his lip. "But if that's the way it went down, where are the goods? Supposing he had an envelope with him, what did she do with it?"

"Lots of places to hide it in that study," DeeDee said. "She could have stuck it between two law books before the judge got downstairs. Or in a credenza drawer. It could have looked innocuous enough. She went back for it later."

"I guess."

"If Trotter was coming through with the promised goods, why'd she shoot him?" Kong asked.

"To tie up a loose end. This is one cold gal," DeeDee replied.

"Funny," Duncan said, "Tony Esteban described her as hot."

"I guess it depends on your point of view."

"I guess it does," Duncan said, matching the bite in DeeDee's voice.

Gerard said, "The key to all this is Napoli. If he sent Trotter to the Lairds' house, and Mrs. Laird was expecting him, we've got ourselves a case of premeditated murder."

"Or," Duncan countered, "it was a burglary gone bad and a matter of self-defense as she claimed." Or, he thought, there was another scenario. The one in which Elise was supposed to die, not Trotter. But he had only her say-so for that, and after his conversation with Esteban, it seemed even more unbelievable than it had before.

"What about ballistics on the two weapons?" Gerard asked.

"I got the report this afternoon," DeeDee said. "Both clean as a whistle. The judge purchased his seven years ago."

"Long before he'd even met Elise," Duncan remarked.

"Trotter's has never been attached to a crime," DeeDee said. "Dead end."

Addressing Kong, Bill Gerard said, "Napoli needs to be found."

"I've got every cop on the force with his eyes peeled and an ear to the ground. Right now, looks like he's pulled a Jimmy Hoffa."

Then the captain turned to Duncan. "What's your next move?"

He thought about it for a moment. "I suppose I go back to Mrs. Laird and tell her that Esteban categorically denied being Coleman Greer's lover. See what she says."

"She'll say he's lying." That from DeeDee.

Gerard spat into his cup. "You're frowning, Dunk. What's on your mind? Something tells me you're not convinced."

He stood up, walked over to the window, and gazed out thoughtfully. A horse-drawn carriage loaded with tourists was clopping past. The tour guide was pointing out the architectural features of the Barracks, giving them its history.

"Convinced?" Duncan said. "Good word, Bill. Because I've been wondering if maybe Esteban was trying to convince me that he's heterosexual. Everything he said, his posturing, it was almost overkill. His Barbie-doll fiancée with an engagement ring bigger and heavier than an anchor. Her jumbo-sized breasts, which he paid for. Eyeballs through his dick."

"Excuse me?"

He turned back into the room and smiled at Kong. "You had to be there. The point is, he wanted there to be no doubt in my mind that he was a superstud, a man who liked women."

"He's that way all the time," Gerard said. "You ever see him when he wasn't strutting his stuff?"

"He's cocky as hell," Kong agreed.

"Yeah, the swagger and boasting may just be elements of his personality." Duncan returned to his chair, but didn't sit down. He braced his arms against the back of it. "But let's say, for the sake of argument, that Esteban and Coleman Greer *were* lovers. Who's the one person in the world who might know about it and could expose it?"

Gerard supplied the answer. "Coleman's longtime friend and confidante, Elise Laird."

"Right. When the concierge of Esteban's building announced me, I said I was there to talk to him about Coleman Greer's friend Elise Laird. Maybe he panicked. Maybe he thought right then and there that the jig was up, that his homosexuality was about to be exposed. So everything he said and did was calculated to contradict anything she might have told me about his relationship with his teammate."

"Or maybe her lie was payback for him dumping her, just like he said," DeeDee argued.

"He's an egomaniac. That whole story about her coming on to him could have been a lie."

She made a snorting sound. "You just don't want her to be guilty of murder."

"And you do," he fired back.

"No," she said slowly. "But just because she's got a doll face and a figure to match doesn't mean she's innocent."

"It doesn't mean she's guilty, either."

"Why don't you push her the way you do other suspects?"

"Up till today she hasn't been a suspect."

"Only because you didn't want to think so," DeeDee retorted angrily.

"Hey!" Bill Gerard interrupted the heated exchange. "What's with you two?"

"Duncan goes calf-eyed every time he sees Elise Laird."

"You're pissing me off, DeeDee." He spoke quietly, his lips barely moving to form the words. "Name one thing I've failed to do." She continued to stare at him without speaking. *"Name one thing I've failed to do,"* he repeated angrily.

She looked across at Bill Gerard and sighed with resignation. "He hasn't failed to do anything. He's conducted a thorough investigation."

"Thank you," Duncan said stiffly. "Have I been cautious? More tentative than normal? You're goddamn right I have. Because we're about to go after a superior court judge's wife. Before we do, I think we should explore every possibility. Because if we're wrong on this, we're gonna be butt-fucked and then we're gonna be unemployed."

A long, tense silence ensued. Kong broke it by saying, "Ouch."

Everyone relaxed, chuckled. But Duncan wasn't quite ready to forgive DeeDee, and when he looked at her, he didn't smile.

"It comes down to this, Dunk," Gerard said. "One of them is playing you. Either Mrs. Laird or Tony Esteban. Who do you think it is?"

That's the question he'd asked himself a thousand times since leaving Esteban's penthouse. Did he believe the cocky baseball player or the woman who had killed a man last week?

Quietly he said, "Elise Laird." He glanced at DeeDee, then addressed his captain. "Too many things about that shooting just don't add up, Bill. It doesn't *feel* right. I think we should get her in here tomorrow, put her in an interrogation room with a court reporter, make it official. Hammer her pretty hard. See if we can shake something loose."

Gerard nodded, but he looked unhappy. "Shit's gonna fly. I'll notify Chief Taylor tonight, because I'm sure he'll get an earful from Judge Laird tomorrow." No one disputed that. "Kong, let them know soon as you get anything on Napoli."

"Will do."

DeeDee was the only one in the room who looked happy. She stood up and dropped her empty soda can in the wastebasket, saying to Duncan, "I'll be at my desk, if you want to go over the plan for tomorrow."

"Fine."

On his way out, Kong nudged Duncan and said in an undertone, "I still want to hear about that eyeball thing."

Duncan was left alone with Gerard, who was using his necktie to polish his reading glasses. "What your partner said, is it true? Do you go moony over this lady?"

"I'd have to be a eunuch not to notice her, Bill. And so would you."

"I've seen her. I understand. So I gotta know. Can you put blinders on and be objective?"

"She's married."

"Not what I asked, Dunk."

"She's a principal in an investigation."

"Again."

"We've got no solid evidence on which to build a murder case against her. Yet. But upon my recommendation we're moving forward on the investigation, and if we find that needed evidence, I'll get an indictment."

Gerard replaced his eyeglasses and reached for a stack of paperwork on his desk. "All I needed to hear."

CHAPTER
15

"ELISE?"

She spun around, knowing she looked guilty. Knowing she was. "Cato," she said, laughing breathlessly. He was standing in the open doorway, carrying a shopping bag. "You scared me. When did you get home?"

"Just now. What are you doing?" As he came into the study, his expression was curious, a shade suspicious.

"This room still makes me jumpy."

"Then why come in here?"

"I was checking the repair."

She indicated the wall that had been patched after the bullet from Trotter's pistol was removed. Yesterday policemen had taken down the crime scene tape and told them they were free to use the room again. Cato had people standing by to restore his study to its pre-incident perfection.

The bloodstained rug had been rolled up and hauled out, with his instructions that it be destroyed. He didn't want it back. Then the entire room had been cleaned and sanitized by professionals.

"I wasn't satisfied with the workmanship and knew you wouldn't be, either," Elise said now. "I was looking in your desk for the plasterer's business card. I wanted to call him first thing tomorrow."

"Mrs. Berry has his business card."

"Oh."

"I'll ask her to reschedule him."

"I think you should. You want the job done right. I know how much you enjoy this room."

"It's sweet of you to care." He smiled. "Join me for a drink before dinner?"

"I'd like that." She came from around his desk and glanced down at the bag. "What's that?"

"A present."

"Hmm." She reached into the pink tissue paper sticking out the top.

"It can wait." He set the bag on the floor, slid his arms around her waist, and tried to kiss her, but she pulled away. "I intended to freshen up before you came home. I rested this afternoon as you suggested, and actually managed to nap. I haven't even brushed my teeth yet."

"I don't mind."

"But I do. I'll go upstairs and make myself presentable. You mix the drinks."

"Even better, I'll mix the drinks and bring them upstairs."

"That is better." She disengaged herself and moved toward the door.

"Here, take the bag with you." He picked it up and passed it to her.

"Can I peek?"

He laughed. "I think you will whether or not I give my permission, so go ahead."

Matching his lightheartedness, she left the room, calling over her shoulder, "Vodka and tonic, please. Lots of lime, lots of ice."

She jogged up the staircase and went straight into their bedroom. As soon as she closed the door, she leaned against it, breathing hard, her heart pounding. She was trembling. She'd come awfully close to getting caught.

Following his confession about hiring the private investigator, Cato had been tender and loving, frequently asking if she had forgiven him for his mistrust. She assured him that he had her forgiveness. Her responses to him were warm and affectionate. On the surface, nothing seemed amiss.

She brushed her teeth and quickly changed into the new outfit wrapped in tissue inside the shopping bag. She was spraying herself with fragrance when he entered the bedroom carrying two drinks. He looked at her and nodded approval.

"The difference was worth the wait."

"Thank you."

"Fit okay?"

"Perfect." Holding the full skirt out at the sides, she did a pirouette.

"Nothing fancy," he said, "but I saw it and liked it."

"So do I. Very much. Thank you."

He had removed his suit jacket and tie. The top two buttons of his shirt were undone. Giving her a meaningful look, he closed the bedroom door. She glanced at her wristwatch. "Mrs. Berry will be waiting to serve dinner."

"I told her to keep it warm, so we can take our time."

He crossed the room and handed her the drink. He clinked his glass of scotch against it. "To forgetting the shooting and its unpleasant aftermath."

"I'll drink to that."

They both took a sip of their drinks, then he pulled her toward the bed, sat down on the edge of it, and guided her to stand between his spread thighs. He set his drink on the nightstand and placed his hands at her waist. "I'm not sure I can wait till you finish your drink."

She took several sips from the glass, then set it on the nightstand beside his.

He moved his hands lightly up and down her rib cage. "Are you still angry with me, Elise?"

"About the private investigator? No, Cato. I've told you time and again. What else could you think? All the signs pointed to an affair. It was silly of me not to explain Coleman's situation to you."

"Even if you had, I wouldn't have approved your meeting him in hotel rooms."

"I didn't inflame his desire," she said with a light laugh. "I tried